D1711347

The Phantom Cottage

Also available in Large Print
by Velda Johnston:

A Howling in the Woods
House Above Hollywood

The Phantom Cottage

Velda Johnston

G.K. HALL & CO.
Boston, Massachusetts
1986

For my sister, Bernita Frier

Published in Large Print by arrangement with
Dodd, Mead & Company

British Commonwealth rights courtesy of
Blassingame, McCauley & Wood

G.K. Hall Large Print Book Series

Set in 18 pt Plantin

Library of Congress Cataloging in Publication Data

Johnston, Velda.
  The phantom cottage.

  (G.K. Hall large print book series)
  1. Large type books. I. Title.
[PS3560.0394P46 1986]   813'.54   86-11941
ISBN 0-8161-4034-0 (lg. print)

One

One afternoon not long ago, I drove twenty miles down the Cape for a last look at that isolated old farmhouse. It sat there in the cup of the low surrounding hills, its roof gently bowed by the snows of at least two hundred years, its brown shingles faded and split and curled by the heat of two hundred summers. Now that the shutters had been opened, multi-paned windows reflected the late afternoon light. That same light gave a bronze tint to the ragged purple lilac bush —perhaps half as old as the house itself—at the right side of the door, and a pinkish cast to the white-blossomed dogwood tree at the left. As I sat there, staring across a stretch of foot-high grass at the house, a nesting robin emerged from the dogwood, made a scolding sortie toward my Volkswagen, and then flew back into her waxy-blossomed shelter.

How peaceful the house looked, basking in the May sunlight! It seemed almost impossible to realize that on a night only a few weeks before, I'd sat bound to a chair in the low-ceilinged room beyond those multi-paned windows, my eyes dazzled by candlelight that seemed to pulse bright and then dim, my ears straining to identify the voice of the person beyond that wavering screen of light. Most of the time during the unmeasured interval in that room, I'd been able to believe I was enmeshed in my own nightmare. It was only now and then that I knew, with a cold sense of doom, that the room was real, and that the dim, changing shape beyond the candle's flicker had killed once, and, if driven to it, would kill again.

Remembering, I shivered. After a moment I switched on the ignition. Backing off the narrow road onto the long grass, I turned the little car around and headed back up Cape Cod toward Garth.

I'd arrived in Garth one April night about a month before, bringing with me from New York one elderly dog, two suitcases, one typewriter, and my sketching equipment. Part of my baggage also was one bruised, if not actually broken, heart.

The man was Kevin Doyle, a Brooklyn-born young law clerk whose father had belonged to the New York City Police Department and whose two older brothers still did. For almost a year I'd hoped that Kevin soon would get around to proposing. Then, one fine spring evening, he told me he'd decided to follow that time-honored formula for instant success. He was going to marry the boss's daughter.

At least he'd had the tact not to choose as the setting for his announcement one of the small Manhattan restaurants where we'd dined on happier evenings. Instead, it was across a table in one of those bustling, brightly lighted midtown steak houses that he said, "Janey, I don't know how to tell you this, except straight out. I'm going to marry Lenore Coombs."

I'd stared at him, my stomach knotting up. True, the blow wasn't entirely unexpected. In the past few months our dates had dwindled from two or even three a week to one. And when we were together, I'd been aware of his frequent silences, and of a perfunctory quality in his love-making.

Still, I'd kept hoping that the reason he gave me for his abstraction—his worry that he might not be promoted—was the real one.

Dark blue eyes holding a look of earnest candor, he said, "I won't try to tell you I'm crazy about Lenore. You know how unlikely that is. You've met her."

I had, one late afternoon when I dropped by the impressive offices of Coombs, Coombs, and Hatfield, where Kevin toiled as the most recently hired law clerk. Lenore Coombs had come out of her father's office a few moments after I arrived, and Kevin had introduced us. She was a thin, nervously talkative girl, probably a little past thirty.

"But look at it this way, Jane. What could we have on what I make, and you make? A one-bedroom apartment, and a two weeks' vacation in Jersey or the Poconos once a year. And it might go on like that for five years, maybe longer." Humility mingled with that candid look in his eyes. "I know I'm no world beater. I was in the bottom third of my class at Columbia. Without old Coombs' help, I might have to wait until I'm bald before they took me into the firm."

I stared down at my half-eaten steak. All right, so I'd been a fool. But from hints he'd dropped, I knew I wasn't the first girl who'd fallen for those dark blue eyes, and the faint brogue that came and went, and that smile loaded with Irish charm, nor would I be the last. (I could imagine him, a few years from now, turning that candid blue gaze on women jurors, as he presented arguments drawn up by law clerks as low-salaried as he now was. He'd go a long way.)

"And I'm thinking of you too, Jane. You deserve someone who can give you more than I can. You're pretty, and talented, and you grew up used to a comfortable life."

Often before he'd contrasted my childhood, as the daughter of a moderately successful St. Louis physician, with his own bleak early years, when his mother had struggled to raise three boys on his polio-stricken father's pension from the police department. In fact, perhaps his childhood reminiscences had been one of the reasons I'd fallen in love with him. All unknowingly, I must have harbored the sentimental notion that the progeny of the poor but honest always grew up with a sound sense of values. The truth, as he'd just demonstrated, was that childhood memories of ill-heated rooms, coarse food, and bill collectors could awaken a greed so impatient that a man might sell himself to the anxious father of a plain young woman teetering on the brink of spinsterhood.

I managed to say, "Thanks for worrying about my future."

He flushed. "I know you must think I'm a heel."

I had no reply to that, at least none I cared to make in a crowded restaurant, and so I said nothing.

He looked at my plate. "You've finished with that? Would you like some dessert? The cheesecake is supposed to be very good here."

I said, in a completely expressionless voice, "Oh, God."

His flush deepening, he signaled the waiter. "All right. I'll take you home."

Later that night I sat alone in my three-room Village apartment, the apartment I'd thought Kevin and I would share for at least the first few months of our married life. Howie lay beside me on the small sofa, front paws and grizzled head in my lap. Usually the sofa was off limits to him, but tonight I felt comforted by the weight of his massive head, and even by his snores. Apparently his pushed-in nose—he's mostly bulldog—makes it difficult for him to breathe. When he's asleep, which at his age is a great deal of the time, he snores, and even when awake he emits faint whistling noises.

Stroking Howie's stiff fur, I decided to leave town for a while. There was no reason I shouldn't. My work—I've written and illustrated three books of verse for children, ages four to seven—could be done anywhere. It was only Kevin who'd kept me tied to New York.

I'd drive up to the town of Garth, on Cape Cod. Not that I'd ever seen it. During my two years in New York, I'd strayed no farther from Manhattan than eastern Long Island and the ski resorts in the Pocono Mountains. But my friend Laura Crane had told me about Garth. (Or rather, I reflected sadly, my late friend—Laura of the lovely face and haunted gray eyes, who'd met death on a dark Manhattan street less than three weeks before.) She'd spent a few days in Garth as a small child, she'd told me, and had never forgotten the ancient saltbox houses, nor the waters of the bay ebbing and flowing over the sun-warmed tidal flats, nor the giant waves smashing against the cliffs on the Cape's Atlantic side.

I'd try to rent a little house near the shore. In early April there'd be plenty of vacancies. I'd bask in the spring sunlight, and write my four-line verses about moths and wood turtles and starfish, and draw my pen-and-ink illustrations.

Living alone would hold no terrors for me, not in that peaceful place. And I'd have Howie. True, the protection he offered was largely illusory. While it would be inaccurate to say he wouldn't hurt a fly—I'd seen him snap at flies as he lay on the fire escape outside Laura's wretched one-room apartment—I doubted that he'd welcome a fight with anything more fierce than a fly. But his horrendous appearance, and the growl that sometimes rumbled like distant thunder in his broad chest, could chill the blood. Children never stopped to pet him on the streets, and many adults shied to the far edge of the sidewalk. Considering his gentle heart, that was rather a pity.

Yes, tomorrow Howie and I would go up to Garth. When I became reasonably sure that the sight of familiar bars and restaurants wouldn't evoke too-painful memories of Kevin, I'd return to the city.

I cried for a while after I went to bed. It really isn't much comfort to tell yourself that someone who's thrown you over wasn't the man you thought he was. The heart still grieves for just that—the man you thought he was.

But there was anger in my sobs, a blessed, saving anger. After a while, with my tears all wept out, I fell asleep.

Two

It was past eleven o'clock the next night when, with Howie snoring gently in the Volkswagen's back seat, I turned a curve in a narrow road and came abruptly upon Garth.

I'd meant to be there much earlier. But that morning it had taken more time than I'd anticipated to pack and to notify my publisher and my apartment house superintendent of my plans. Lunch at a restaurant in the upper reaches of the Bronx took another half hour. Then, in midafternoon, as I drove along the parkway through Connecticut's April-green hills, rain began to fall. As it grew heavier, the balky windshield wiper, wheezing across the glass in a smeared arc, forced me to slow to thirty miles an hour. The rain slackened just after I crossed the Rhode Island border, but by then it was already getting dark.

In Providence, with its traffic and its five-street intersections and flashing signals, I lost all track of the signs pointing to the parkway, and had to take an alternate route out of town. On this neon-blighted highway—Renee's Cocktail Bar, Jim's Giant Hamburgers, Hillhaven Funeral Home, Carson's Motel—I stopped in the graveled space before a darkened Gifte Shoppe, hauled an old picnic hamper from the trunk, and took out Howie's dish, a can of dog food, and a can opener. He ate beside the car, uncomplaining in the faint drizzle. As for my own dinner, it could wait. I was eager to leave the garish mainland behind and cross the canal to the Cape.

Perhaps it was only the appearance of Cape Cod on the map—that long arm, bent at the elbow, its fist half-clenched against the gales that in winter come howling down from the Arctic Circle. But anyway, I felt that on the Cape I'd find myself in a different world—quiet, even austere, but soothing in its very aloofness to a visitor with a bruised heart and a shaken self-esteem.

Every once in a while, something lives up to your expectation of it. The Cape *was* a different world. Soon after I crossed the canal and began to drive up the old Cranberry Highway, the last of the drizzle gave way to a wispy ground fog. It hovered in the hollows of the almost deserted highway and swirled between the black-trunked pines like smoke—or like the wraiths of those long dead. Well, I reflected, if any part of this nation was haunted, the Cape should be. Not just by Indians and Puritans, but by European seafarers—Vikings and later the Portuguese—who long before America had a written history must have been driven to their deaths on the Cape's shoals. I recalled reading that the Pilgrims, lingering on the Cape for three weeks before they sailed on to Plymouth Rock, had found a skeleton whose still-undecayed blond hair evoked the fierce Norsemen in their longboats.

Perhaps, I reflected with a smile, those white veils winding through the wet black tree trunks were ghosts of my own ancestors, curious to see their midwestern-born descendant. According to my mother, her people had lived on the Cape early in the eighteenth century, until the loss of their meager resources, invested in the cargo of a merchant ship that never returned, had set them to moving westward.

I passed through villages. Most of the old houses, set back from elm-shadowed streets, were already dark, although now and then a window showed the bluish glow of a television set. Except for an occasional neon sign marking a motel or a tavern, the small business districts were also dark. I'd driven about ten miles past one of those quiet villages when my headlights bathed a roadside sign. Garth was two miles away, along the next road leading to my left.

Although well-paved, the side road was so narrow that the arching trees almost met overhead. Now and then I seemed to catch a whiff of salt air. That might well have been the case since, according to my road map, only about five miles of land separated the ocean from the bay at this point on the Cape's forearm. I turned a bend in the road and there, abruptly, was Garth.

Slowing, I approached it with dismay. At its edge, a low frame building displayed a blue neon sign, *Steve and Grace's Tavern*. As I passed its broad front window, I saw the revelers in the brightly lighted interior—apparently middle-aged and quite staid revelers of both sexes, seated at the long bar. But beyond the tavern the street sloped darkly away. There was nothing to indicate a motel, and no lawn signs advertising rooms for tourists.

As I drove slowly down the main street, I saw that Garth was not like the towns lower on the Cape. No fine old houses here, set far back on gracious lawns. Instead the houses were small, with only scraps of picket-fenced ground separating them from the sidewalk. I was sure that by daylight those little cottages must hold a certain miniature charm, but right then I was too tired and hungry to appreciate it. I rounded a slight curve in the street, and there ahead was a wooden sign, jutting out at right angles from a three-story frame building and illuminated by an old-fashioned, metal-shaded electric light. The sign said: *Garth Hotel. Open All Year. Gabe Harmon, Prop.*

Parking at the curb, I climbed to the hotel's veranda. Shades had been drawn at the glass double door, but light seeped around the edges. I pushed the bell at one side of the door, waited, rang again.

Footsteps. The door opened, and a man said, after a moment, "Yes?"

I blinked in the light from the lobby

14

behind him. "I'd like a room, please." When he didn't answer, I said, with some asperity, "This is a hotel, isn't it? And you are open all year, aren't you?" I could understand why he might be somewhat startled by a young woman arriving alone late at night during the off-season. But still—

He opened the door wider. "Come in."

I stepped into an austerely plain lobby, furnished with a few old leather armchairs and settees, two potted palms and a semicircular registration desk. He stepped behind the desk and turned a cloth-bound register around for my signature. He was quite young, I saw now, perhaps twenty-six. Probably his hair normally was near the light brown color of my own, but the same sun which had tanned his face had bleached yellow streaks in his thick straight hair. His nose was as self-assertive as Joe Namath's, but otherwise his features were acceptable enough. His eyes were blue and held a deadpan look.

"I can't give you a room with a private bath. I'm having all those rooms done over."

Not we. I. "Then you're Mr. Harmon, the proprietor?"

"Yes. Why?"

"That sign with your name on it looks at least fifty years old."

"No need to change the sign. My grandfather and father had the same name."

Evidently it was true that New Englanders used words as if they cost money. I signed the register, "Miss Jane Warren, New York City," noticing as I did so that the last guest, a J. J. Hornsmith of Boston, had checked in nearly a month before.

Gabe Harmon turned the register around, looked at my signature and then at me, and said, "You'll find a bath two doors down the hall from your room."

"All right. I have my dog with me. Where can he sleep?" If Howie had been a dainty poodle or Yorkshire, I might have asked to keep him in my room. But even the most genial of innkeepers, which this one certainly wasn't, might draw the line at Howie.

"We keep a pallet on the porch off the dining room. Your dog can sleep there. I'll get your luggage."

I followed him out to the car. "My typewriter is on the floor behind the front seat." As he opened the rear door, Howie raised his mashed-in visage and blinked.

"Don't be afraid," I said.

"I'm not afraid."

Howie was wagging his stump of a tail now. But that didn't mean anything. He's like Will Rogers. He never met a man he didn't like.

Gabe Harmon handed me the typewriter and then gathered the rest of my luggage from the car's trunk. With Howie following, we returned to the lobby. My host set my luggage on the floor. "I'll bed your dog down, then show you to your room." He snapped his fingers. "Come on, boy."

Howie's ugly, mournful face swung toward me. "Go on. It's all right." Obediently he trotted after the man.

When Gabe Harmon returned to the lobby, I was studying the row of framed presidential photographs that hung along one wall. Theodore Roosevelt, Taft, Harding, Coolidge, Hoover, Eisenhower, and Nixon. No Wilson, or F. D. Roosevelt, or John Kennedy. Not even gaps where their photographs should have hung.

Gabe said, "Granddad and my father were Republicans." He paused and then added, "Rock-ribbed." There was just the trace of a smile in his eyes.

"Obviously," I said, liking him a little better.

He took a key from the rack behind the desk. As I followed him up the stairs, I asked, "Could I possibly get something to eat? I've had no dinner."

"The housekeeper and her husband are still watching Johnny Carson, I imagine. I'll ask her to scramble you some eggs."

The second-floor room into which he showed me was austere but clean, furnished in golden oak, and with a straw carpet on the floor. He said, laying the key on the dresser, "I'll tell Mrs. Dudley about the eggs. They ought to be ready in fifteen minutes."

"Thank you. Oh, another thing. I'd like a bath before I go to bed. Will there be hot water?"

"Yes, if you let the tap run long enough." He started toward the door and then turned around. "By the way, how long will you be staying?"

"At this hotel? Just tonight, if I can find a small cottage to rent tomorrow. I'd prefer something near the water."

"Plenty of cottages. The person to see is Senator Carberry. He owns a little all-year house on the bay side that ought to be about right for you. And he's agent for other rentals around here."

"A senator? And a real estate agent?"

"State senator, although everyone knows he still hopes that Washington will be calling any year now." Again that faint smile appeared in his eyes. "Anyway, he keeps his real estate office open in the summer and on weekends when the legislature is in session. Well, come down as soon as you're ready."

When he'd gone, I took off my coat, washed my face at the basin in one corner of the room, and renewed my lipstick. Then I descended to the lobby. Not knowing which door to try, I opened the one through which he'd led Howie, and found myself in the dining room. All but a few of the small square tables were stacked with upended chairs. One near the entrance, however, had been set with a paper mat, filled water glass, and knife and fork. Through the glass upper pane of a swinging door I could see a gray-haired woman standing beside a stove. As she turned away from it, our eyes met, and she gave me a pleasant smile.

I sat down at the table. A few moments later Gabe came through the swinging door, a metal tray bearing a plate of scrambled eggs in his hands. He crossed to the table and then stopped short. The plate slid across the tray, halting against its raised rim.

I looked up. His gaze was riveted on the bracelet, once Laura Crane's, that encircled my left wrist.

Earlier that evening I'd thought of the fog wisps drifting between the tree trunks as ghosts. But it was Gabe Harmon who looked as if he were really seeing a ghost. There was shock in his eyes—and something else. Grief? Remembered pain? Anger? I couldn't be sure.

But one thing I did know. Laura had lied to me. Garth wasn't just the town she'd visited for a few days as a small child. She'd lived here as an adult, and this man had known her, and now had recognized her bracelet.

He'd recovered. He placed the scrambled eggs before me. "Look all right?"

"Fine." Then, swiftly: "Why were you staring at my bracelet?"

"Well, it's very unusual."

"Yes." I looked down at it, a slender jade dragon with ruby eyes, coiled around my wrist on a wide gold band.

"Mind if I ask where you got it?"

"A friend gave it to me."

I might have added, "My friend is dead. She called me one night, sounding frightened, and asked to come to my apartment, but on the way there, she was killed."

Tonight, though—tired out and burdened with a new hurt—I didn't want to talk of Laura and her shockingly sudden death. Besides, he'd played it cagey, implying that he stared at the bracelet only because it was unusual. I could be cagey, too.

"Anything else? Coffee?"

"Thank you."

In silence he served the coffee, nodded good night, and went through the door into the lobby. When I crossed the lobby five or ten minutes later, there was no sign of him.

Up in my room, I took a dressing gown and slippers and a fresh cake of soap from my suitcase and went down the hall until I found a door labeled *Bath*. The tub was something left over from the Ark, claw-footed, and only about four feet long. No matter. The water from its tap, only a lukewarm trickle at first, became a steaming cascade. I soaked luxuriously for about fifteen minutes, then dried myself on a worn-thin bathtowel labeled, mysteriously, *Grenville Arms Hotel*, put on my robe and slippers, and returned to my room.

Something was different. Oh, yes. Those two folded pink blankets across the foot of my bed. Someone had come in and placed them there while I was bathing. Then, instinctively, I turned to the dresser and saw that something else was different.

Before leaving the room, I'd taken off my bracelet, snapped it shut again, and placed it on a little metal tray obviously designed to hold collar buttons, bobbie pins, and knickknacks. Now the bracelet lay, open, near the dresser's edge.

Picking it up, I turned it so that the light fell on the letters engraved inside, "J.L. to L.C."

She'd never told me who J.L. was, nor had I asked. Almost from the first, Laura had somehow made it plain that she'd accept me as a friend—the one friend she had—only as long as I didn't ask questions.

Obviously Gabe Harmon couldn't be J.L. But it was equally obvious, I reflected with rising anger, that he'd been so eager to make sure that this bracelet had been hers that he'd sneaked in here to look at its engraving.

The bracelet made a clinking noise as I dropped it onto the tray. If this kept up, I told myself grimly, I'd soon be a manhater. And for a girl who'd always considered the male sex not only attractive, but singularly likeable, that was an unhappy fate to contemplate.

After turning my room key in its lock, I looked at the thumb latch for a moment and then shoved it into place.

Three

Perhaps it was the coffee. Perhaps I was just too tired to sleep. Anyway, for a long time after I went to bed, I lay awake thinking of Laura Crane. All around me was the silence of the little town where she must have lived once and where something or someone, I felt sure, had put that haunted look in her eyes.

I'd first seen her one steaming night of the previous July in a Greenwich Village restaurant, Peter's Grapevine. On warm evenings in spring and early fall, the out-door tables at Peter's, set under a huge, ancient grapevine, are filled with rich-looking girls and their escorts. But in midsummer the rich girls are all away—in Easthampton or Europe—and Peter's prices

come down, and tourists and summer bach-
elors and even parties of typists dine at
the tables beneath the grapevine's writhing
branches.

That night I'd been supposed to dine at
Peter's with Kevin, but work on a brief had
interfered. (In those days, I'm sure, it really
was work that made him break a date
occasionally.) Reluctant to prepare even
soup and a sandwich in my tiny kitchen on
that sweltering night, I'd gone to Peter's
alone.

The diners were only a handful—a lone
middle-aged man, two couples sitting in the
companionable silence of the long-married,
and, over against the brick garden wall, a
dark-haired girl with a plate of spaghetti
and meat sauce before her. Fleetingly I
noticed that she must be a year or so
younger than myself, twenty-two perhaps.

The waiter led me to another table
against the wall, only a few feet from the
brunette girl's table. It was only after I'd
given my order that I looked over and saw
that she was cover-girl lovely, with an oval
face, set with great dark eyes, between the
silky falls of dark hair. But she'd done
nothing to enhance her beauty. No eye
shadow or mascara. No foundation makeup

25

on the ivory skin. She wore pale lipstick, but I sensed that was only because she feared she'd appear freakish without it.

By contrast, the dog who lay beside her chair on the worn bricks was the ugliest I'd ever seen. The face was English bull, with a mashed-in nose and protruding tusks. But the pointed ears were too long for a proper bulldog's. So was his body. Its length and coarse fur indicated German shepherd blood, and its colors—white, black, dirty yellow—hinted at collie. The stubby tail, like the face, was bulldog.

He was so ugly—and his bloodshot eyes were so gentle and friendly—that he went straight to my heart. Without thinking, I said, "Hiya, fellow."

That was a mistake. With rheumatic stiffness, he heaved himself to his feet and took a step toward me.

"No, Howie!" The girl caught at his collar—an expensive one, I noticed, set with brass studs. She threw me a resentful look. "Stay!"

The dog lay down. At that moment the waiter placed onion soup before me. I spooned it, eyes fixed on the brown earthenware bowl. On Park Avenue, I'd seen owners of five-hundred-dollar poodles or

Afghans jerk their pets away from contact with the friendly noses of ordinary dogs or the friendly smiles of people. But usually owners of mixed-breeds aren't so exclusive.

Feeling rebuffed and even a little hurt, I kept my gaze averted from the girl all through my soup and veal parmegiano and salad. Why hadn't she left? Surely she must have finished her main course by now. And yet no waiter had approached her.

Finally I looked at her. Her fork was poised over the still-unfinished plate of spaghetti, and her gray eyes, filled with remorse, were looking at me. Oh, Lord, I thought. One of those sensitive souls. She'd seen she'd offended me, and now she couldn't even finish her dinner.

Her chair scraped over the worn brick. Leading the dog, she came and stood beside my table. Fleetingly I noticed the lovely and unusual jade bracelet encircling her wrist. "I'm sorry," she said. "I didn't mean to be unpleasant. It's just that Howie is all—I mean, I don't have any—"

She broke off, a flush dyeing her face. I felt embarrassed color in my own cheeks. With those few stumbling words she'd revealed her loneliness, a loneliness so stark, so complete, that she was jealous of

27

her dog. It seemed to me that I could feel the loneliness blowing from her like a chill wind.

"Oh, that's all right." Then, swiftly: "I have an idea. You haven't had coffee yet, have you? Let's have it together."

She hesitated for a long moment, and then sat in the chair opposite me. The dog lay down beside her. I signaled the waiter. "Do you want dessert?" I asked, every inch the brightly chattering hostess. "I seldom have dessert. Calories."

"No, I don't want dessert."

When the waiter had left coffee and gone away, I said, "So your dog's name is Howie."

"It's Howard, really. I found him on Howard Street during that last big snowstorm. He was trying to get under a parked car." Her accent made it sound like "paaked caah." She added, "With no collar."

"So you took him in. Was that all right with your apartment house superintendent?"

She smiled faintly. "At my apartment house nobody objects to anything. It was the only place I could find."

"I know how that is. But I was lucky.

When I came here over a year ago, a friend of mine, another St. Louis girl, had just decided to go back home. So I got her apartment."

"Well," I added, "I suppose we might as well introduce ourselves. I'm Jane Warren, and I live on West Twelfth Street."

"I'm Laura Crane. I came here from Denver a few months ago."

Oh, no, you didn't, I thought. Not with that accent. At least, she hadn't grown up in Denver.

"My place is on Eighth Avenue. It's really just a housekeeping room. I was twenty-two last month, and I work in the mailing room at Macy's."

She'd spoken rapidly, with an air of great openness. But I sensed, from the guarded defiance in her gray eyes, that in effect she was saying, "Accept it or not, this is all I intend to tell you about myself."

Then the last thing she'd said caught at my attention. The mailing room at Macy's. Surely she could get a better job than that. Any number of firms would be glad to have her decorate their outer office, even if all she did was to say, "Mr. Whozis will see you now."

But already I knew better than to make

any comment about her job. Instead I said, "That's a nice dog collar."

Until we'd finished our coffee, we discussed Howie's grooming, diet, and rabies shots. Pleased to be the center of attention, he kept his muzzle resting on his extended paws and coyly rolled his bloodshot eyes from one to the other of us.

At last I said, "Are you doing anything the rest of the evening?"

After a moment she answered, in a small voice, "No."

"Well, neither am I. So why don't we go to my place for a while and talk?"

Her eyes were both wary and eager, and again I sensed her terrible aloneness. At last she said, "All right. Could I bring Howie?"

"Of course. My super doesn't object to dogs. He has two of his own."

"We'd better stop off at my place and get his blanket. He's shedding a lot."

Her apartment was dreadful. Up three flights, with garbage cans on the landings, and coming through the closed doors the sound of brawling couples, wailing children, and booming TV sets. She had a lumpy-looking daybed, one straight chair and a battered black plastic armchair, and a cooking alcove with a gas plate and ancient sink. As I watched her moving about— shaking the dog's khaki blanket, emptying his dust-scummed water dish into the rusty sink—I found it almost incredible that a lovely and apparently refined girl should be living in such squalor.

My own modest three rooms, when we reached them, seemed almost embarrassingly palatial. I turned on the hi-fi set my parents had sent me for my birthday and poured out two glasses of Madeira left over from the last time I'd cooked *veal au Madeira* for Kevin. We settled down to typical girltalk—clothes, movies we'd seen or wanted to see, and the handsome bracelet on her wrist. When she offered to let me try it on, I saw the engraving inside, but made no comment. Looking up, I saw from the expression in her face that by my silence I'd passed some sort of test.

Later I showed her photographs of my parents and older brother back in St. Louis, and of Kevin. She made appreciative comments, but produced no snapshots of her own from her handbag, and mentioned no boy friends.

When she rose to go, I said, "Why don't we have dinner again sometime soon, and maybe go to the movies afterwards?"

31

Again that half-eager, half-reluctant pause. "I'd like to. But I can't afford places like that one tonight very often. I—I went there tonight because I thought it would be nice to eat in a garden." She pronounced it "gaaden."

"I can't afford it either." Even old hands in the children's book field are seldom rich. It was only a small legacy from an aunt that enabled me to have my VW and splurge occasionally on a meal at a fairly good restaurant.

From then on we frequently had dinner together, in some inexpensive restaurant, or at my apartment. (To my relief, she never even suggested that we have dinner at her place.) It was obvious she had no other friends. And, for all she mentioned it, one would have thought she had no past, that she'd been born the week she came to New York and rented that dreadful room. On the other hand, it was only once that she threatened to retreat into her complete solitude.

That September night we were dining thriftily off spaghetti and meatballs in a Village Horn and Hardart's. A fraternity brother of Kevin's, I told her, wanted me to find him a date for Friday night. She laid her fork down on the thick plate. "No."

"Why not? He's nice, Laura. I've met him. And he and Kevin are going to try to get theater tickets for whatever we want to see."

Her face was white, angry. "I don't want to date anyone!"

I felt too taken aback to say anything at all. She went on, in a let's-get-this-straight tone, "I never intend to marry. So why play around? Why get involved?"

I itched to lean across the table and shake her. At the very least I wanted to say, "Who's asking you to get involved? It's a date, that's all. And as for never marrying, that sounds silly and childish—even sick. Perhaps you should talk to a psychiatrist."

But if I'd said that, or even hinted at it, she would have walked out of the Automat and back into the life where she had no one but Howie. Her eyes told me that quite clearly.

"Okay, Laura." I forced a smile. "It's your life. I won't try to tell you how to run it."

We continued to share Dutch-treat dinners and movies— more frequently, in fact, as my dates with Kevin became fewer. Laura must have been aware of my increasing unease about Kevin, as well as my increasingly free evenings. But she made no comments, perhaps out of tact, perhaps because she felt, in view of her own reticence, that she had no right to.

As it turned out, Laura and I shared Christmas. Kevin and I had planned to spend Christmas Eve in my apartment, with a tree, and have dinner the next day in Brooklyn with his family. Two days before Christmas he told me it was all off. His Boston aunt, who was gravely ill, was coming home to Brooklyn for what might be her last Christmas. Under the circumstances, his mother felt that he should spend both Christmas Eve and Christmas Day at home, with only the family present. Now I realize that he must have spent Christmas Eve, and perhaps part of Christmas Day, at the Coombs estate in Dobbs Ferry. Even then, his story struck me as odd, but I had to accept it.

And so Laura and I cooked a small turkey Christmas Day in my apartment. Before dinner, I presented my gifts—a manicure set for her and a plastic bone for Howie, on which to exercise his few remaining teeth. She handed me a box beautifully wrapped in gold paper with a chartreuse bow. Inside was the jade dragon bracelet.

"Laura, I can't accept this!"

"Why not? You've always liked it."

"But it's valuable!" I held the box out to her. "I don't know much about jewelry, but surely this is worth at least two hundred dollars."

She looked almost angry. "I don't want it." With both hands, she pushed the box toward me. "I want you to have it. I've decided," she said obscurely, "that there's no *point* in my keeping it."

I looked at her feverishly intent face. "All right. Thank you more than I can say." I clasped the odd, lovely thing around my wrist.

After our Christmas dinner, we went to a movie matinee. The setting was Scotland. When we emerged from the theater, light snow was falling through the early dark. "Oh, how I'd love to see Scotland!" I said, as we moved along Greenwich Avenue. "It must be beautiful."

Perhaps it was the snow, its falling white flakes gilded momentarily by the light from street lamps and shop windows. Perhaps it was the nostalgia of some past Christmas, clutching at her heart. Anyway, she made one of her rare revealing comments.

"The movie reminded me of Cape Cod, especially around Garth. The little cottages, I mean, and the sea pounding against the cliffs. And there are marshes up there, you know, and lots of ponds."

I ventured a question. "Did you ever live there?"

"No," she said after a moment, "we were just passing through."

That was absurd, of course, as a glance at the map proves. Nobody "passes through" Cape Cod. Where would you pass through to? She herself must have realized the absurdity, because moments later she amended, "I mean, when I was little we once spent a week of our vacation there. Then we went on up to Maine."

At the corner where she turned off toward Eighth Avenue, I said good-by to her and walked home through the thickening snowfall, with the jade bracelet heavy and unfamiliar on my wrist.

Less than ten weeks later, she was dead.

The telephone's ringing dragged me up through layers and layers of sleep that March night. I drew it to me and said groggily, "Hello."

"Can I come to your place, please?

Someone—something's—I can't stay here."

Laura's tone, thin and taut, brought me wide awake. "Are you in danger? Shall I call the police?"

"No! It's just that I came home from a late movie and—I'd better leave now."

I glanced at the clock. Twelve-forty. "Take a cab, if you can get one." Especially in the less prosperous neighborhoods, cabs are scarce after midnight.

"All right." She hung up.

I rose, slipped on my robe, and made coffee, wishing I had some brandy to offer her. She'd sounded as if she might need it. I pictured her leaving that fetid apartment house and hurrying through streets where cars were few and taxis even fewer.

Twenty minutes passed, twenty-five. Even if she hadn't been able to take a cab, she should be ringing the buzzer any moment now.

Ten more minutes passed, while the coffee turned cold on the stove. Perhaps something had delayed her departure. Perhaps, strange girl that she was, she'd even changed her mind. Going into the bedroom, I dialed her number. No answer.

Should I call the police? No, she'd rejected that idea with a vehemence that suggested she'd never forgive the arrival of the police at her place. Start out to look for her, then? Not knowing whether she'd started up Eighth Avenue or Seventh, I might well miss her. I pictured her on my apartment house doorstep, futilely pushing the buzzer and growing more upset by the second.

I'd wait a few minutes more. Going into the living room, I switched on the TV picture but not the audio, and stared at stock cars, one with Mickey Rooney at the wheel, racing soundlessly around a circular track. Finally I glanced at my watch. More than an hour had passed since her call.

With a sudden, cold certainty that something terrible had happened, I started for the phone. In spite of that vehement "No!" I was going to call the police.

The phone rang before I reached it.

He was one of the new breed of police, calm-voiced, courteous. There'd been a hit-and-run accident on Eighth Avenue nearly an hour ago. The victim was Laura Crane, according to her social security card. They'd found a small address book in her handbag, but except for mine, all the names and numbers were those of business firms, a hairdresser, a dry cleaning shop, and so on.

I found my voice. "Is she—is she—"

"Yes, Miss Warren. It must have happened instantly." He paused. "Can you tell us how we might reach her family?"

"No. She never mentioned having any. She once told me she came from Denver. That's all I really know about her, except that she worked at Macy's."

"We'll check with the Denver police, and with Macy's too, of course." Again he paused. "Will you come down and identify her?"

Who else was there to do it? "You mean right now?"

"No. Ten o'clock tomorrow will be all right." He gave me the address.

A little after ten the next morning, lightheaded from lack of sleep, I looked down at a long table in a white-tiled, glaringly bright room. "Yes, that's Laura Crane," I said, and turned away. Those few seconds had been bad, but not as bad as I'd feared. Her face hadn't been altered. Whatever her injuries had been, they were hidden by the long sheet and by the bandages swathing her head.

A police lieutenant had met me in the

building's lobby and accompanied me into the tiled room. In my shocked state, I never thought to ask whether or not he was the officer who'd called me the night before. He might have been. He was equally polite, and quietly sympathetic.

In the little anteroom I said, "Have you learned anything more about her?"

"No. The Denver address she gave Macy's was fictitious. The Denver police are still checking to see if there are any missing girls of her description. We'll let you know if we turn up anything."

"Have you found the driver of the car?"

"No, and there's a good chance we never will. There were only a few witnesses at that time of night—a cook in an all-night hamburger stand, a couple of cleaning women coming home from work, and a bum who was apparently looking for a doorway to sleep in. Their stories disagree. One of the cleaning women says the car was a black sedan, and the other says it was a dark green station wagon. The bum says the car ran through a red light. The cook says the girl went against the light and stepped off the curb right into the car's path."

Had she, quite deliberately? Had whatever frightened her last night increased her secret burden to the point that she could no longer live with it? No, it was far more likely an accident. She'd been hurrying along, much too distressed to be careful of traffic—

The lieutenant was saying, "We found a dog in her room."

Howie! I'd forgotten all about him. "What became of the dog?"

"He's at the SPCA, I imagine. That's what usually happens in these cases."

I'd find him, I decided instantly, and take him to live with me.

"It's a pity," the lieutenant went on, "a lovely young girl like that. But since there's no one to claim the body, I guess—"

"I'll claim it," I said, before he could finish the sentence. "If you could—could just tell me what—"

"I'll give you the name of a mortician. You tell them how much you want to spend, and they'll handle everything."

Kevin managed to get away long enough for the brief service in the funeral home's chapel. To my almost tearful gratitude, so did two girls she'd worked with in the mailing room. They'd scarcely known her, one of the girls said. She seemed to sort of shy away from everyone. Still, everybody sort of liked her.

Kevin hurried away to an appointment after the service, and the girls had to return to work. I alone accompanied Laura out to the hastily bought plot in the far reaches of Queens, and said a silent prayer beside her grave.

I'd thought that was the end of Laura in my life, except for Howie, of course, and the bracelet she'd given me. But now, staring toward the invisible ceiling, I reflected that it was almost as if her restless spirit had led me to this little town, past those prim cottages she'd mentioned to me, and into this hotel, whose owner she had known.

Or, to put it less fancifully, perhaps it wasn't just because I'd always heard that Cape Cod was quietly and austerely beautiful, exactly the place for a young woman to recover from a jilting. Perhaps I'd sensed, when she mentioned Garth last Christmas, that it was her home, the place that held the key to the puzzle that was Laura.

The puzzle of Laura. A puzzle that seemingly had been smashed, beyond hope of anyone's solution, by a speeding car on a New York street.

For the first time, it occurred to me that her death might have been neither an accident nor suicide.

I stared for a few minutes longer into the dark. Then, succumbing to all those hours I'd spent at the VW's wheel, I turned over in bed and fell asleep.

Four

I opened my eyes to midmorning sunlight streaming through the net curtains onto my bed and the straw carpet. From somewhere came the sound of hammering, and the whine of a power saw. For a second or two, I didn't know where I was. Then I thought, with an odd mixture of excitement and obscure anxiety, "I'm in Garth, Laura's town." This morning, somehow, I felt sure of it. This was the place from which she'd fled to wrap herself in icy loneliness in a New York slum. Quickly I got out of bed and dressed.

When I descended to the lobby, I found Gabe Harmon standing behind the semi-circular desk. A certain tension in his stance made me think he'd been waiting for me.

"Good morning." His smile was brief, impersonal. "Did that noise on the third floor wake you?"

"No, I think I just woke up. I don't suppose there's any chance of breakfast at this hour."

"If you'll settle for orange juice and cornflakes and coffee."

"Gladly. Has my dog made any trouble?"

"No. He's still out there on the porch. I gave him some meat scraps for breakfast. Was that okay?"

"Usually he doesn't have breakfast, but it's all right. I'll just give him less tonight."

Going into the dining room, I crossed to a glass-paned door in the opposite wall. Yes, there was the enclosed porch. Howie lay on what had once been a crib mattress, sleeping off his unaccustomed meal. Turning, I walked back to the table I'd occupied the night before. A few minutes later the kitchen door opened and Gabe carried a tray to me.

"Mrs. Dudley's busy upstairs," he explained. "Don't eat those sliced bananas on the cornflakes, if you don't want to."

"I'll eat them. I'm famished."

"I phoned Senator Carberry. His little house over on the bay is available for a month. After that it's promised to some friends of his. The Senator's office is in his house, and it's outside of town. I'll drive you over there, if you like."

And extract a little information on the way. Well, that was fair enough. There were a number of questions I intended to ask him.

"Thank you. I know you must have had breakfast, but would you like to keep me company with a cup of coffee?"

"Sure," he said after a moment. Going into the kitchen, he came back with a cup and saucer and sat down opposite me.

"I want to thank you for the extra blankets you put in my room."

He tensed slightly. I half expected him to say it was the housekeeper who'd brought the blankets. Instead he said, "It turns cold here at night."

"You also looked at the engraving in my bracelet, didn't you?"

He flushed, but his blue gaze didn't waver. "It might have been some crazy coincidence, you turning up here in Garth with the same kind of bracelet. I had to make sure it was Laurabelle's."

"Laurabelle! Her name was Laura, Laura Crane."

"No," he said quietly, "if she gave you that bracelet, her name is Laurabelle Crandall. I've known her nearly all my life."

"Here? In Garth?"

He nodded. "I was six when she and her mother and aunt came here. Laurabelle was about two. Her mother died less than a year later, but Laurabelle and her aunt stayed on."

"They'd come here from Denver?"

He stared at me. "Whatever gave you that idea? They were Canadians. Ottawa, I think."

So Denver was a hometown she'd plucked out of the air, just as she'd plucked a name with the same initials as her own.

He asked, "Where did you meet her?"

"In New York."

"So that's where she ran off to."

"You didn't know?"

"No one did. February a year ago she just disappeared. She left a note for her aunt saying she'd get in touch, but she never did." He paused. "Is she still in New York?"

I found I couldn't answer—not when I didn't know what, if anything, she'd meant to him.

He must have read the answer in my face. He said in a flat voice, "Then she's dead."

"Yes."

"Somehow I thought she was, when I saw that bracelet on your wrist." Looking down at his coffee cup, he turned it in its saucer. "How did it happen?"

"A hit-and-run accident. Three weeks ago, on Eighth Avenue."

"God! Poor little Laurabelle. But at least it's better than—" He broke off.

"Than what?"

"When you told me she was dead," he said reluctantly, "I thought of suicide."

My voice was sharp. "Why? Had something happened here? Something that made her unhappy?"

"No." There was reserve in his tone. "At least, not that unhappy."

"Then why—?"

"After she left," he said reluctantly, "there were the usual stories floating around. I thought maybe things had gotten—just too tough for her."

"You mean, there were stories that she was pregnant?"

He nodded. And who, I wondered, was supposed to be the man?

"She wasn't when I met her," I said, "and I don't think she had been. Call it feminine intuition, if you like, but I feel sure of it."

"Where is she—?"

"A cemetery in Queens. I arranged for it. She seemed to have no one else." I paused. "I'm sorry. Apparently you were fond of her."

He smiled faintly. "Considerably more than that, a couple of years ago. But that wasn't unusual. I guess every male in town, from sixteen to sixty, was in love with Laurabelle at one time or another."

"And she?"

He stared at me. "You mean, you were friends, and yet she never told you?"

"She told me very little, and even that, apparently, wasn't true. For instance, the one time she mentioned Garth—that was last Christmas—she said she'd spent only a week here, as a child. I never questioned her. She made it clear that if I did, she'd just—withdraw. She was a strange girl."

"Strange?" His forehead wrinkled. "I'd never have called Laurabelle strange. Of course, she did read poetry, and was crazy about animals, and had always been on the quiet side. But even so, she was friendly enough, in her shy way. Nearly everyone liked her."

A popular, quietly friendly small-town girl. How to reconcile that with the withdrawn, haunted girl I'd known?

"Of course," he went on, "she changed somewhat after she got mixed up with Jules. She must have known the whole town was talking about them, and that made her a little—defensive."

"Jules?"

"Jules Laretta. He was the one who gave her the bracelet, the one I was sure she must have told you about." His faint smile looked wry. "He's also the one who beat me out with Laurabelle.

"You'll meet Jules," he added. "You'll meet everyone, if you stay here more than a few days. In the off season, this is a very small town." He paused. "I suppose you'll want to see Mrs. Newcombe right away. She's Laura's aunt."

Heart sinking, I said, "I suppose I'll have to. She'll want to bring Laurabelle back from—"

"Yes," he said quickly.

"What's she like?"

"Mrs. Newcombe? What my mother used to call standoffish, but otherwise all right. Pays her taxes, keeps her place up, contributes to all the rummage sales, and so on. But about your seeing her. Maybe Dr. Rainey ought to break the news to her. You see, she had a stroke about a month ago."

My dismay deepened. It would have been hard enough to tell her of her niece's death under any circumstances. But to confront an invalid with news like that—

"It was only a slight stroke, and I hear she's recovering nicely. But still, maybe Dr. Rainey ought to break the news, before you give her the details." He paused. "If you like, I'll call him right now and see what he thinks."

"I'd appreciate it."

He went through the door into the lobby. When he came back, about ten minutes later, I was sipping the last of my coffee.

"I told Doc Rainey the whole story. He'll talk to her this afternoon. He suggests that you go to see her at four o'clock."

"All right."

Again he gave that wry smile. "Maybe I should have warned you. Before dark everyone in town will know about Laurabelle, and that you were a friend of hers."

"You mean the doctor's a gossip?"

"Oh, I suppose he sticks to his Hippocratic oath—guards the secrets of the consulting room, and so on. But otherwise, he's the town crier. Well, I'd better get upstairs and see how the carpenters are getting along. We'll go over to see Senator Carberry right after lunch. Okay?"

"Fine."

He gathered up the plates and carried them to the kitchen. Going out to the little porch, I aroused Howie from his gorged slumbers. He followed me across the dining room and lobby and out into the street.

Yes, I'd been right. On such a sunny day, I didn't need a coat over my plaid wool suit. From the glove compartment of my car, still parked at the curb, I took Howie's leash and snapped it to his collar. We set off along the slightly curving street.

There was a boating equipment store next to the hotel. Drawn blinds concealed its windows, and its door was padlocked. At least half the business establishments on the street—gift shops, antique shops, a beauty parlor, a dress shop—had closed for the winter. Some bore window signs simply stating that fact. Others said breezily, "See you next June. Have a good winter," or, "We're off to our Miami shop. Drop in on us down there." But other places were open—a drugstore, two groceries, a bank, and a small drygoods store with flowery Easter hats in the window. Across the street, I noticed, was a fairly new red brick building with the words *Town Hall* spelled out in brass letters above the doorway.

People passed, looking with friendly curiosity at Howie and me. Some said, " 'Morning." Others merely smiled and nodded. At first I was startled. Strangers, neither in New York nor St. Louis, greet each other on the street, and I certainly hadn't expected the supposedly clannish Yankees to do so. But, as I smiled in answer, I found I liked the custom.

The stores gave way to the little frame houses I'd passed in the dark the night before. As I'd guessed, they were charming, with their clapboards painted white or pale blue or green, and their prim gossip benches facing each other on the small front porches. They'd be even more attractive when the flower gardens behind the picket fences, now showing only the green blades of tulips and daffodils, were in bloom.

Again I wondered why the houses here were so small and close together. Suddenly it occurred to me that perhaps these cottages had housed crew members of the old whalers and merchant ships. Shipowners and captains, with a position to keep up, must have built big houses like those I'd seen lower on the Cape and those I glimpsed on Garth's side streets. But the crew members chose a neighborly closeness, so that their wives and children wouldn't be lonely during the long months the men were away.

Beyond the houses, another row of shops stretched toward the tavern at the end of the street. Vaguely aware that a woman was coming toward me, I turned and looked at a display of shoes in a shop window.

The woman had stopped beside me. After a moment I became conscious of the odor of alcohol. Turning, I found the woman staring at my left wrist. She looked up at me, and I felt distinct shock. Her reddish brown eyes were filled with hatred.

She was a big woman, at least five-foot-ten, and somewhere in her middle years. Her hair, whatever its original shade, was now bright red. It made the enraged pallor of her face all the more pronounced.

Her hatred couldn't have been directed toward me. I'd never seen her before. It was the sight of Laura's bracelet that had enraged her. Feeling chilled and even, absurdly, a little frightened, I turned and pulled Howie away. Walking more quickly than before, I started back to the hotel.

Almost everyone had liked Laurabelle, Gabe Harmon had said. Well, I'd just seen someone who most definitely hadn't liked her.

As long as I was in Garth, I decided, that bracelet would remain in my suitcase.

Five

Gabe didn't join me for my excellent lunch of creamed ham on toast, served by the pleasant-faced Mrs. Dudley. But when I emerged from the dining room into the lobby, I found him waiting. "Ready?"

"Yes," I said. "Shall we go in my car? You'd better drive."

He nodded.

With Howie in the back seat, we drove out of town, along the highway that led toward the outermost reaches of the Cape. Scraggly pitch pines bordered both sides of the road, now and then giving way to a field still green with winter wheat.

"There doesn't seem to be much farming up here."

After a moment he said, "Soil's too thin."

I glanced at him, feeling rebuffed. At breakfast he'd seemed communicative, even loquacious. Now he'd reverted to the taciturn, poker-faced man of the night before.

At last I asked, "Is there anything wrong?"

He didn't parry with "What do you mean?" His blue eyes shot me a side glance. Then he said, "After you left the hotel, I played back our breakfast conversation in my mind. I'd been too shaken up by the news about Laurabelle to notice it at the time. But you weren't telling the truth. You said you hadn't known Laurabelle came from Garth."

I said, a bit angrily, "I didn't know. I believed her when she said that she'd spent only a week up here years ago."

"Then how is it that you show up here, soon after her death?"

I'm not one to wear my heart on my sleeve, especially a bruised heart. "I wanted to find someplace quiet and peaceful for a while. I'd always wanted to see the Cape, anyway. And Laura's mention of Garth had stuck in my mind."

"And you're able to do that? Just leave your job anytime you like?"

"Lord! You are suspicious, aren't you? I brought my work with me." I explained then about my little nature sketches and their accompanying verses.

He said after a moment, "Okay, I'm sorry."

"Apology accepted. But now I have a bone to pick with you. You weren't exactly the genial innkeeper last night. In fact, for a moment or two I thought I was going to have to sleep in my car."

"I know. I'm just not cut out to be a resort hotelkeeper. When I saw you standing there, looking every inch the New York career girl, I thought, 'Damn it all, they're starting up here already.' "

"They?"

"The summer people. Even when I was growing up, a few of them were pretty bad. But now! Why, last summer I rented a few third-floor rooms to half a dozen college sophomores. One night they and almost fifty of their friends threw beer cans and bottles down into the street without opening the windows first. And these weren't yippies or potheads, mind you. Just nice, clean-cut, semi-alcoholic products of the best middle-class families."

I suppressed a smile. "I hope their

families paid for the windows."

"They did. But I still wish I'd kicked the seats of those Bavarian leather shorts most of them were wearing."

"You know what you are? You're a young fogy."

For the first time, I heard him laugh. "I suppose so. Anyway, I'm getting out of the hotel business. That's why I'm remodeling. I want to find a buyer."

"What will you do then?"

"Go to New York. Get a job."

"You know New York?"

"I graduated from Columbia."

I tensed. "Law School?"

"Engineering."

"Oh."

He threw me a curious side glance and then went on, "I came back to the hotel after college only because Dad was failing. He needed my help. But now that he's gone—he died last summer—I'm getting out."

"Well, you should have no trouble finding an engineering job."

A bluejay flashed ahead of us across the road. Last week in New York, I'd sketched a jay teetering on a pine bough, beak parted in a raucous jeer. I hadn't written the accompanying verse yet. But it would be something like, "Here's a notorious prankster and thief, impudent beyond belief, sports a coat of policeman blue—" No, it didn't scan.

As if he'd caught a fragment of my thoughts, Gabe asked, "Did you show Laurabelle those animal books of yours?"

"Of course." I thought of her curled up on the floor beside the low bookcase in my apartment, one of her rare smiles curving her lips as she turned the pages of *Zoo Families*.

"I'll bet she liked them." His voice sounded as if his throat had tightened. "Laurabelle loved anything that flew, or swam, or had a leg on each corner."

Impulsively, responding to his tone rather than his words, I said, "I'm sorry."

He looked at me and then returned his gaze to the road. "Perhaps I'd better make something clear. I was fond of Laurabelle. Hell, we were kids together. But I wasn't still—emotionally involved with her. I hadn't been for more than two years."

Hadn't he? The way he'd reacted to the sight of her bracelet the night before had made me feel he was "emotionally involved," in one way or another. Anyway, why was he taking the trouble to assure me he wasn't? Because he wanted me to know he was heart-whole and fancy-free? That would be a flattering assumption, especially to a girl who'd been stood up, if not at the church door, then practically at the engagement ring counter. But he'd given me no other reason to think he was attracted to me.

We'd turned off the highway, along a road traversing low ground covered with marsh grass, from which flocks of meadow-larks kept rising on their triangular wings. Ahead, on a rounded hill studded with junipers, rose a red brick Georgian house, its white pillars gleaming in the afternoon sun.

"That's Luke Carberry's place."

"Is he rich?"

"No. He has just his salary and whatever he makes from his real estate agency. His grandfather built that house, back in the days when his family did have money. Luke Carberry is the last of one of the oldest families on the Cape."

"Is he a good state senator?"

"Good enough. He hasn't absconded with public moneys, or anything like that. Anyway, we've kept sending him back to the legislature for twenty years. We're loyal to the old families around here."

"Twenty years! And he still thinks he might be elected to Congress?"

"Congress, hell. Oh, he'd settle for Congress for a term or two. But he's actually our local Harold Stassen. His hope springs eternal."

"You mean he wants to be *President?*"

"Yes, and when you see him you'll understand why he thinks he could be. If ever a man looked like a President, Luke Carberry does."

Two stone pillars flanked the graveled drive. On the right-hand one, brass letters said, "Cedar Hill." On the other, similar letters spelled out, "Senator Lucius P. Carberry." Not State Senator. Just Senator.

A gray Chrysler stood in the circular turnaround at the foot of the broad front steps. Leaving the VW parked behind the Chrysler, we mounted to the cool shadowy porch. Carberry himself opened the door to us. I knew he couldn't be anyone else. He was over six feet tall, with a mane of snowy hair and a noble-looking head which, even though he wore horn-rimmed glasses, instantly reminded me of those busts of Roman senators in New York's

62

Metropolitan Museum.

He said, beaming, "Gabe, my boy! Good to see you. Come in, come in." Then to me, as we stepped into a wide, well-polished hall, "You must be Miss Warren, the young lady from New York."

When I'd shaken his wide, soft hand, he led us into a book-lined study off the hall. "Sit down, sit down." He himself sat in a leather chair behind a big mahogany desk. "I hear you befriended the Crandall girl in New York. Terrible thing about her, terrible!"

He took off his horn-rims, as if finding them misted over, and rubbed the lenses with a white handkerchief. His general appearance was so pompous that, for an instant, I suspected him of making a politician's gesture meant to indicate concern. Then I saw that his hands trembled slightly. He really had been shocked by the news.

Almost every Garth male from sixteen to sixty, Gabe had said, had been in love with Laurabelle at one time or another. Lucius Carberry appeared to be still under sixty.

"I heard about it when I went to the post office about an hour ago to get my copy of the *Congressional Record*." Gabe caught my eye, and I recalled his saying that Dr. Rainey would spread the news all over town before dark. "I suppose," the Senator said to me, "that you came up here to see Laurabelle's aunt."

I was tired of explaining that I'd known nothing of Laura's aunt, and very little about Laura, until I came here. "I'll see Mrs. Newcombe this afternoon. But afterwards I'd like to stay up here for a while."

"So Gabe told me. If you're looking for peace and quiet, Miss Warren, there is no place like the Cape in the off season. In fact, there is no place like the Cape at any season. Now I know that love of homeland is considered old-fashioned these days." As people usually do when making that highly debatable statement, he spoke in a tone of defensive melancholy. "But I'm not ashamed of it, nor do I feel there is shame in praising the particular spot in our nation where one was born. And the Cape is indeed worthy of praise. Our ports, from which our ancestors put out to brave the South Pacific gales. Our ocean and bay, teeming with fish. Our people, many of them worthy descendants of those who took up their abode in the American wilderness more than three centuries ago. In fact, I am humbly proud to be one of those descendants."

He paused. Finding no adequate answer, I murmured something about always having wanted to come to Cape Cod.

Probably he made that speech on the floor of the legislature at regular intervals, and then sent printed copies to his constituents. He was impossible—a windy, platitudinous bore. And yet I sensed the sincerity of his loving pride in the Cape and in his own ancestry. The appearance of his house and of this room, with a framed reproduction of the Massachusetts Bay Colony charter hanging on the wall behind him, indicated such love and pride.

"And if you decide upon the little bayside cottage I'll show you, you'll enjoy Cape Cod at its finest. The sunsets, Miss Warren, the sunsets!" He added, in an entirely different tone, "The off-season rental is forty dollars a week, payable in advance. The place is available for only one month. After that it's promised to some friends of mine for the whole summer. Blankets come with it, but not linens. Perhaps Gabe will rent you some."

"Forty a week seems quite a lot."

"I might make it a little cheaper, since

you're a single person. Anyway, let's go look at it. I'll lead the way in my car."

We went out to the driveway. Accompanying us to the VW, Lucius Carberry looked in the open rear window and then gave a braying laugh. "That's the homeliest dog I ever saw!"

About the only thing Howie seems to resent is being laughed at. Thunder rumbled in his broad chest. The Senator's hand, reaching inside the car, hastily withdrew.

"He's not angry," I said. "Just hurt. But he'll get over it."

As if to confirm my words, Howie wagged his tail. Gingerly Carberry reached in and patted the wide head. "Why, he likes me." From his gratified tone, I guessed he was one of those who believe dogs have an infallible instinct as to who is worth liking.

"Well," he said, turning away, "follow me."

As we trailed the Chrysler down the road toward the highway, Gabe said, "I'll loan you the linens. I didn't want to say so in front of the Senator."

"Afraid you'd lose your standing as a hardheaded Yankee?"

66

He smiled. "Something like that."

When we reached the highway, the Chrysler led us a mile or so toward Garth, and then turned right down a narrow dirt road. There were no houses along here, just stands of pitch pine and still-leafless oaks, now and then giving way to meadows brown with knee-high wild grass. In one meadow weeping willows, their fragile branches still more yellow than green, leaned like long-haired dryads above a pond. At an intersection, we turned left for about half a mile along another dirt road, then right along one that was little more than tire tracks.

It ended in a wide space between two sand dunes. As we pulled up beside the Chrysler, I had my first view of Cape Cod Bay. The tide was out. Beyond the wide clean beach the tidal flats, festooned with amber and purple kelp, glistened in the afternoon sun. The Senator got out of his car. Gesturing to the right, he said, "There's your little hideaway."

At first sight, I loved it. Not that it was in any way quaint. Set on stilts, it was just a rectangular box, surrounded on three sides by a railed sun deck. But instantly I thought of looking through that wide front window each evening at the tidal flats, shimmering with multi-colored sunset light.

With Howie toiling after us, we climbed the broad plank stairs. The living room, paneled in knotty pine, was furnished in typical summer cottage fashion—white wicker tables and chairs, and a battered bookcase beneath the front window. The bedroom held a knotty pine bed, with what felt like a good mattress, and a matching chest. The pots and pans in the kitchen might have first seen service in a Spanish-American War mess tent. But they'd do. In fact, the only thing that bothered me was that the back kitchen door opened directly onto a ten-foot drop to the sand below.

A storm last fall, Senator Carberry explained, had badly damaged both the front and rear staircases. So far, he'd managed to replace only the front staircase. "People don't realize how expensive it is to be a landlord," he said, in a tone appropriate to one of the Hundred Neediest Cases.

When we returned to the living room, he told me that he'd had the light and gas turned on last week in case an early tenant appeared. "You can have the phone hooked up this afternoon. The company office is in Town Hall."

"Yes, I'd need a phone." I was scanning the battered volumes in the bookcase. With delight I saw that some of them were the sort of second-rate classics I'd heard of all my life, but never read—*Quo Vadis?*, and *Seventeen*, and *The Last Days of Pompeii*.

Then, as I raised my gaze to the window, I realized I could do something else I'd heard of all my life. Growing up inland, I'd never cooked dinner on an ocean beach. I'd buy a bag of charcoal along with my other supplies—

Somewhere not too far away a dog yipped. Other dogs joined in, forming a noisy chorus. Beside me, Howie made an alarmed sound, half whine and half growl, and the coarse hair stood up along his spine.

"Don't be frightened," Carberry said. "It's that pack of wild dogs back in the swamp. They never come out onto the beach. Apparently the hunting is good enough back there that they don't have to."

Wild dogs! I stared at him. He didn't seem the sort to put a visitor on. Visitors, after all, sometimes became permanent residents—and voters.

Gabe must have noticed my expression. "It's true. Some vacationers adopt a dog for the summer, and then, when they leave the Cape, turn the dog out on its own. Over the years a considerable pack of abandoned dogs has formed back there in the swamp.

"And of course," he added, turning to Carberry, "there were the dogs that escaped from the Manwell Refuge during the SPCA raid two years ago. Some of them must have joined up with the pack. Come to think of it, Laurabelle was the one who caused that raid."

I said, startled, "Laurabelle!"

"Yes. About six years ago a retired nurse named Mary Manwell started an animal shelter on her property, a couple of miles outside Garth. She built a high wooden fence around the kennels. When people went there to leave a dog or adopt one—a contribution was expected in either case—they were never taken back to the kennels. You'd tell her what sort of dog you wanted, and this assistant of hers, a mentally retarded fellow, would bring out several for your inspection."

He went on to explain that stories began to circulate. Stories of sick animals inadequately treated, dead animals left unburied. At last, unable to bear the stories, Laura had gone out to the refuge one night, scaled the high fence, and looked around with a flashlight. What she'd seen had sent her to the county authorities. "I don't imagine they were too happy to hear that the rumors were true. In small communities, people don't like to take legal action against each other. But finally the SPCA raided the place one night. In the confusion some of the dogs escaped. The others were taken to an animal shelter down the Cape, and Mary Manwell's place was closed by court order."

"What became of her?"

"Oh, she's still around. Some people wanted to see her indicted, but others felt she'd done the best she could, on what little money she had, and with no one but that retarded fellow to help her. In the end, no legal action was taken."

"She's drinking heavily these days," Carberry said. "A member of one of our oldest families, too. It seems a shame."

Drinking. That woman in front of the shoe store this morning. "Is she a large woman, red-haired?"

Gabe's eyes were alert. "Yes. Why?"

"I think I saw her on the street this morning." I paused. "Where is that swamp?"

"You can see it from the back window,"

Carberry said.

We walked into the kitchen. From its window I could see a stretch of marshy ground, covered with tall, plumy-topped reeds. Beyond the marsh was a large stand of pitch pine. From the midst of the pines a few taller trees—black oaks or maples, probably—raised leafless branches.

"The swamp's quite a way in," Gabe said, "where you see the tops of those hardwood trees. It's called Joshua's Swamp. Two hundred years ago a sailor named Joshua got lost in there and was drowned."

"Just last summer," the Senator said, "the two-year-old son of a Philadelphia couple wandered in there and was attacked by dogs. Fortunately the searchers found him before he was seriously bitten. True, the dogs might not attack an adult. But I advise you, Miss Warren, not to go in there at night or at any time alone."

Somewhere in the depths of the trees a dog yipped. Howie made that worried sound. "It'll be all right," I soothed. "Just stay out of there. And," I added to the Senator, "so will I."

In fact, the idea of once-friendly dogs turned savage frightened me more than would have the idea of naturally wild animals lurking there. Betrayed by humans, they'd swiftly regressed through perhaps a million years, back to a time before the first wolflike animal tentatively approached those two-legged creatures, cooking the day's kill before a fire-lighted cave mouth.

With a slight shudder, I turned back toward the living room.

Six

The Senator and I settled finally for a rental of thirty-five a week. After all, I too have Yankee blood. When I'd written out the check, I glanced at my watch and exclaimed, "I almost forgot my appointment with Mrs. Newcombe! Does she live far from here?"

Gabe said, "In Garth. Look, Senator, suppose you drop me off at the hotel. Then you can lead Miss Warren to Mrs. Newcombe's house."

For a few seconds Carberry looked so upset that I expected him to refuse. Then he said, with forced-sounding cordiality, "Glad to."

In Garth, the Chrysler let Gabe Harmon off in front of the hotel, led my VW along two blocks of the close-packed houses, and turned right onto an upward-slanting street. Instantly the character of the town seemed to change. Here the frame houses, all of them dating from the Victorian era or earlier, were two or three stories tall, and set on sizeable plots.

The Chrysler slowed. Carberry's arm emerged, and his index finger pointed across the street at a bay-windowed house of dark red siding. He gave me a back-handed wave and then sped on down the street. One would almost think, I reflected, as I stopped my own car at the curb, that he was afraid of Laura's aunt. I thought, too, of the way his hands had trembled as he removed his glasses earlier that after-noon.

I'd crossed the street and started up a cement walk when the door of the dark red house opened. A man carrying a small black bag hurried toward me down the veranda steps.

"Miss Warren?" I nodded. "I'm Dr. Rainey."

Perhaps because Gabe had called him "the Town Crier," I'd expected him to be small, elderly, and roly-poly, with bright, inquisitive eyes. Instead he was tall and thin, dark-haired, and probably in his late forties.

"I've broken the news to Mrs. Newcombe. She took it quite well. She's a brave woman." At least, I'd been right about his eyes. They studied my face with open curiosity. "No need to ring the doorbell. You can go right in. She's in the living room."

"Is there anything I should be—careful about?"

"No, don't withhold any details. She wouldn't want you to. I wish I could stay for your interview with her," he said, and I was sure he did wish it. "But I'm already late for a call in the next block. Well, good-by, Miss Warren."

I climbed the front steps, opened the right half of the double front door, and stepped into a narrow hallway. After the bright sunlight, it seemed dim and unpleasantly chill. Ahead, on my right, was a square archway. After a moment's hesitation, I walked to it and found myself looking into a big room, filled with heavy nineteenth-century furniture. Because the shades had been partially drawn at the windows, the room was almost as shadowy as the hallway.

A woman of fifty-odd rose from a straight-backed chair of brown plush. "Oh, please don't get up!" I said.

Ignoring that, she walked toward me, and extended her hand. Her handshake was cool and dry and firm.

Instantly I saw the family resemblance. Like Laura's, her hair was dark, except for a plume of white running back from the broad forehead. Her eyes were gray and wide-set, her nose straight, her mouth wide. But the eyes held a singular coldness, and her lips were thin. Unlike Laura's rounded one, her chin was so square it looked almost masculine. Except for a slight droop at the right side of her mouth, her recent stroke had apparently left no visible mark.

"I'm Adele Newcombe. So you're Laura-belle's friend. Come in, please, and sit down."

I took the chair she indicated, another highbacked plush one. Between my chair and hers stood a marble-topped table. On it was a smiling photograph of Laura, in the cap and gown she must have worn when graduated from her high school. The girl in the picture looked younger than the one I had known, and a great deal happier, but she was undoubtedly the same girl.

"Dr. Rainey tells me my niece died instantly." Her voice was calm. A brave woman, Dr. Rainey had said. But surely even a brave woman, told only that day of her niece's death, would show more emotion than this. One might have thought her completely unconcerned.

"Yes, the police said it was instantaneous."

"Tell me about her life in New York."

"There isn't much to tell. She had a job at Macy's, and an apartment in the Village." No need to speak of that appalling room. "We had dinner together frequently, and sometimes went to the movies. As far as I know, she had no other friends."

"Tell me about the night she died." I became aware that the stroke had left at least one other mark. She lisped slightly.

"She called me around one in the morning. Something or someone had upset her, perhaps even frightened her. She asked to come to my place. On her way there, she was struck by a car. The police never found the driver. At least, they hadn't by the time I left New York."

She leaned forward, as if to pounce. "How is it that you didn't get in touch with me immediately?"

Surely Gabe Harmon had explained all that to her doctor, and the doctor in turn had explained it to her. Perhaps she wanted confirmation of it.

"She'd never mentioned you to me, Mrs. Newcombe. I knew almost nothing about her, not even her right name, as it turned out. But two days ago I decided, for—for personal reasons, to get away from New York for a while. I recalled that Laura— Laurabelle—had mentioned this part of the Cape as a lovely place where she'd spent a childhood vacation. That was the only reason I came here. It wasn't until Gabe Harmon recognized the bracelet she'd given me— But I suppose Dr. Rainey told you about that."

She nodded. "You're not wearing the bracelet."

"No." I wasn't going to mention my brief and wordless and yet upsetting encounter with Mary Manwell. In fact, something about this house, and about Mrs. Newcombe, made me want to end this interview as soon as possible.

"What reason did Laurabelle give you for having run away from Garth?"

Was she trying to trip me up? Or had the

stroke addled her wits? "She never told me she'd run away," I said as patiently as I could, "from Garth or anywhere else. She just said she 'came from Denver.' Aside from that, which wasn't true, she told me nothing of her past, or even her personal feelings, except—" I broke off.

"Except what?" How alert and quick she was. No sign of addled wits now.

Wishing I hadn't started that phrase, I said reluctantly, "Well, once I asked her to go out on a double date. She said that she never intended to marry, and wanted nothing to do with men."

"That's a laugh," Adele Newcombe said, and—unbelievably—laughed. "It was because of a man she left town. For almost a year she'd been trying to get Jules Laretta to marry her—and him married fifteen years to another woman! I tried to reason with her, but it was no use. Her mother was like that, too. Soft-headed where men were concerned." She paused. "You mean that she gave you the bracelet he'd given her, and yet didn't tell you about him?"

"Not a word." How wretched Laura would feel if she knew that her aunt was telling me things she herself had kept from me.

And then another thought struck me. I said, aware of a certain coldness in my voice, "An unhappy love affair might be sufficient reason for a sensitive girl to go away. But why should she break all ties with you and with her home town, and even change her name?"

Perhaps in response to my tone, Mrs. Newcombe's eyes grew colder. "I don't know. All I know is she came home one afternoon looking pale as death. I was sure she'd been with Jules. The next day, while I was taking a nap, she sneaked out of the house and boarded a bus for the Lower Cape. I never heard from her again."

"Did you notify the Missing Persons Bureau?"

"No. What would have been the use? I couldn't have made her come back, if she didn't want to. She was of age. And according to the note she left, she never wanted to see Garth again."

She paused, and then added, "I hear you paid all the funeral expenses. I'll repay you, of course."

No mention of whether or not she intended to bring Laura back from that Queens cemetery. "Very well. The bills are in New York. I'll send them to you." I rose. "I'm afraid I must leave now. I've rented a little house on the bay for three weeks, and I must lay in some groceries."

She, too, rose and moved with me toward the archway. "Did you rent Luke Carberry's place? I saw his car stop outside for a second or two just before yours did."

"Yes, I rented his house."

Stopping, she laughed and turned to face me. "What a fool that man is! He was crazy about me once. Wanted to divorce his wife—she was alive then—and marry me. Of course, that was before he got the political bug. After he decided to run for the legislature, he turned into a model husband, at least in public."

It seemed an odd thing for a woman of her years, and coldly dignified appearance, to tell a stranger. Perhaps, even if the stroke hadn't affected her intelligence, it had dulled her emotions, made her less sensitive to the effect her words and actions had on others. I'd heard that happened sometimes. Or perhaps he'd aroused in her a malice so strong that she couldn't pass up any opportunity of ridiculing Luke Carberry. For instance, if she'd seen her erstwhile wooer eyeing her lovely young niece—

I said good-by to her and with a sense of relief walked out to my car. It wasn't until I made a right turn at the next corner that I realized she'd made no mention of the rumor that Laura had been pregnant. Surely it wasn't delicacy that had kept her from bringing up the subject and questioning me about it. Perhaps she felt sure it wasn't true. Perhaps, in spite of her denial, she knew the real reason Laura had left Garth, a reason that might have nothing whatever to do with an unhappy love affair.

Well, one thing was certain. I wouldn't try to learn anything more about Laura from her aunt. The less I had to do with Mrs. Newcombe, the better. Making another right turn, I headed toward Main Street.

At the Town Hall, I arranged to have the phone turned on in the little beach house. Then I went to the grocery store and spent a pleasant half hour buying everything from salt to soup mix and detergent to dog food. Finally, I went to the hotel to pay my bill and get my luggage.

When I entered the lobby, I found Mrs. Dudley behind the desk, and my typewriter and one of my suitcases beside it. Gabe, she explained, was up on the third floor with the carpenters. "He told us you were checking out, so my husband's started to bring down your luggage." She lifted a paper-wrapped parcel onto the desk. "And here are the linens Gabe asked me to pack for you."

"Thank you very much."

I'd just paid my bill when I became aware that a gray-haired man with a thin, stern face was descending the stairs. He carried my sketching case and my other suitcase. Mrs. Dudley said, in a distinctly nervous voice, "Miss Warren, this is my husband."

"How do you do, Mr. Dudley?"

Pausing at the foot of the stairs, he gave me an unsmiling nod. "You want me to put your things in your car?"

I said, feeling chilled, "Yes, please."

When he'd gone out, his wife said hurriedly, "You mustn't take the way he acts personally. It's the Crandall girl he disapproved of. Garth has as many goings-on as any other town, but Laurabelle and Jules were so *open* about it. And two years ago my husband joined this awfully strict church." She named one of the more rigid Protestant sects. "When he heard this morning what had happened to Laurabelle,

84

he said—" She broke off, flushing.

I suggested gently, "That it was the Lord's judgment upon her?"

"Something like that."

"Well, don't worry about it, Mrs. Dudley. I can understand why some people might feel that way. And I don't take it personally."

It was past five when I drew up beside my rented house. Already the beach and the tidal flats beyond were taking on the warm tones of near-sunset. I'd have to hurry unless I wanted to cook my beach dinner in the dark.

Followed by Howie, and cradling one of my three boxes of groceries in my arms, I climbed the plank steps. I'd set down the groceries and taken out the key Senator Carberry had given me, when someone said, "Hi!"

I turned. He stood at the foot of the steps, round, smiling face upturned, glasses glittering in the late afternoon light. His hair was brown, and trimmed to a short stubble. He was in his early thirties, and— to judge by that round face—might have a weight problem later on. But right now, in gray flannels and a red turtleneck, he looked trim enough.

I said, a bit hesitantly, "Hello."

"Moving in?" I nodded. "You and your husband going to be here long?"

"A month. But just me. I'm not married."

He gave me a wide grin. "Notice how quickly and subtly I found that out?"

"Well, quickly, at least."

"Have you got more stuff to carry up?" When I hesitated, he said, "Look, my name's Bill Brockton. I'm a marine biologist at Woods Hole, I hike along this beach every chance I get, and I'm a nice guy. Besides, your dog ought to keep any guy in line. Is he as vicious as he looks?"

"Worse. But I can control him. And I do have a lot of things to carry up."

He not only toiled up and down the steps several times, but placed my suitcases in the bedroom and my typewriter and sketching case beside the living room bookcase. He asked about those two items, and I explained about my work. Later, as we stored canned goods on the open shelves above the small kitchen range, he talked of his own work. He'd majored in marine biology at Harvard, and later studied for his Master's and his Ph.D. at the University of California. For a little more than two years he'd been attached to the Marine Institute at Woods Hole, on the lower part of the Cape.

"Should I call you Dr. Brockton?"

"Not if we're going to be friends. Do you know the Cape well?"

"I don't know it at all."

His round face beamed. "Then maybe you'll let me show it to you, starting with Garth. What a history! In comparison, Dodge City and Tombstone were staid communities. Three hundred years ago Garth and Provincetown were hangouts for traders and fishermen from all over Europe. They'd drink and gamble and carouse for weeks on end, scandalizing the towns lower on the Cape. They hunted whales right from the shore, putting out in longboats—"

Breaking off, he pushed up the baggy sleeve of his sweater and looked at his watch. "Good Lord! I'm due in Eastham in fifteen minutes—and my car's parked on a side road nearly a mile down the beach."

I felt a twinge of disappointment. He was so nice that I'd thought of inviting him to share my beach dinner. "Look," he said, "how about my picking you up around eight tomorrow night? We'll go to the tavern in Garth. It isn't like three hundred years ago, but it's interesting. Local people mainly, but a few off-Capers who've spent the winter up here for one reason or another."

"I'd love to go."

"Good. See you then."

From the front window, I watched him striding off toward the north. Then I fed Howie, and after that changed into wool pants and my heaviest sweater. Hastily I packed one of the cardboard grocery cartons with matches, charcoal, the paper Mrs. Dudley had wrapped around the linens, a small steak cut in two sandwich-sized pieces, two buns, a shelf from the oven, a long cooking fork, and a thermos of coffee. On top of all that I placed a square of clean white canvas I'd found folded on one of the storage shelves. That would be my tablecloth. With Howie ambling awkwardly ahead of me, I carried the box down the plank steps.

The tide was in now. Under the sunset light the sand was pinkish beige, the water like iridescent satin. I set down the box and, with Howie, started off down the beach in search of kindling. At the water's edge sandpipers skittered ahead of us, retreating before each wavelet, and then, as it withdrew, chasing it to snatch small creatures from the wet sand with their sharp beaks.

Driftwood was everywhere, ranging from tiny slivers, almost weightless in the hand, to great logs. In the dunes' shadows, the satiny gray wood took on an ice-blue shade. Everywhere else, it reflected the mauves and pinks of that magical sunset light. Deciding upon a campfire for after dinner, I picked up large pieces as well as kindling-sized ones. Then, breathing hard under the weight of my booty I returned to where I'd left the grocery carton.

Scooping out a hole in the sand, I filled it with crumpled paper, scraps of driftwood, and the fat little black pillows of charcoal. With a big kitchen match, I set fire to the paper.

To my anxiety, at first only the driftwood burned, sending a plume of fragrant smoke straight up into the windless air. Perhaps, tyro that I was, I'd made some fundamental mistake. After a while, though, the little black pillows turned gray at the edges. When all the coals were caught, sending out a red glow now that the sunset light had faded, I placed the grill over the sandpit, cooked one piece of steak to medium rare, toasted both halves of a bun, and assembled my sandwich.

Never, never—not even at the famous and shudderingly expensive restaurant to which Kevin had taken me soon after we met—had I tasted anything so delicious. Thinking "Calories be damned," I made a second sandwich.

Only one thing marred our picnic. Howie, I discovered, was strictly a city dog. Oh, he'd seemed to enjoy our walk up the sunset-dyed beach. But when the dark began to thicken, he became as uneasy as some Times Square hanger-on transported to blackness unrelieved by traffic lights and neon signs. With small, whimpering noises, he crowded close to me. Not even bits of my sandwich could quiet him for long. And when a brief chorus of barks arose from that stand of pines and hardwoods beyond the reedy marsh—how dark it must be in among those trees at night!—he whimpered piteously and pawed my leg.

"They won't come out here, you sissy." Then, with exasperation: "Oh, all right. You can go into the house. I'm going to build a campfire."

With a speed unusual for him, he scrambled up the stairs ahead of me. I spread his pallet in the bedroom, added a car coat to my heavy sweater and pants, and returned to the beach. The charcoal was still glowing. I piled wood on it—first small pieces, then larger ones—and sat down on the blanket.

It was fully dark now. Gradually a sense of timelessness, of being in touch with things that do not change, crept over me. Even a thousand years ago, adventurers whose names were lost to history must have kindled driftwood fires on the beach, and smelled its fragrant smoke, and watched the glowing sparks make their brief upward flight into the blackness.

Now the fire was almost too warm. Moving my blanket a few feet away, I lay down and looked up at the sky, swarming with stars on this moonless night. I could recognize the Dipper and follow its pointers to the Pole Star. But what was that brilliant star in the east, almost halfway up the black dome of the sky? Sirius? No, I'd heard that in this hemisphere Sirius was a fall and winter star. And what were those six stars arranged in a pattern that suggested a long-fuselaged passenger jet? Perhaps somewhere I could get hold of a star map—

Quite suddenly, I felt sleepy. I scattered

the glowing embers of my fire and covered them with sand. I packed my picnic paraphernalia in the cardboard box, and shook out the blanket. As I climbed the steps, the box in my arms, I realized with pleasurable surprise that I hadn't thought of Kevin more than two or three times that day.

7

Steve and Grace's Tavern, the next evening, confirmed the impression I'd gained of it the night I drove into town. With its harsh fluorescent light, long bar, and bare wooden tables, it looked about as cozy as a railroad waiting room on a branch line. But if its décor was bleak, the spirits of its customers were warm. Even before Bill Brockton had opened the door, I'd heard a babble of talk and laughter, accompanied by Johnny Cash's voice on a juke box.

Heads had swiveled as we came in. Bill led me down the bar, introducing me. Our hosts, Steve and Grace Sandstrum, who reached large hands across the bar to shake mine, and who looked so much alike—both fair and tall and big-boned—that they might have been brother and sister rather than husband and wife. Ruth and Howard Simpson, a middle-aged couple who'd sold me my groceries the day before. A Miss Carruthers—plump, late forties, determinedly blonde—who ran the local beauty parlor. At one of the bare tables sat a quiet-looking gray-haired couple named Aldrich. They were retired Philadelphia schoolteachers, Bill later told me, who'd come to the Cape for the summer five years ago, and then settled down here.

By their expressions—polite, but curious and a shade reserved—I knew that all these people had heard of me, and of my connection with Laurabelle Crandall.

At one of the tables, Bill and I ordered Scotch and water. Even before our drinks came, he began to talk enthusiastically about the Cape. The high, storm-battered cliffs facing the Atlantic along Nauset Beach. The sand dunes up near Provincetown, "like something out of a North African movie." He wanted to show me those places, he said, but couldn't right away. "I'm due at a marine biology symposium down at Cape May tomorrow afternoon. I'll drive down to Hyannis, and fly from there. But when I come back a couple of weeks from now, I'll show you every-thing you haven't seen in the meantime."

Soon after that Dr. Rainey came in, nodded smilingly to Bill and me, and took a seat at the end of the bar, facing the door. At first I felt surprised. Somehow one didn't think of a doctor as a frequenter of bars, especially one as bleakly ordinary as this. Then I realized that for one of his gossipy inclination—he probably thought of it as a keen interest in human nature—this would inevitably be a favorite spot. Proba-bly more news was exchanged here each night than the local paper carried in six weeks.

About half an hour later, the tall, red-haired woman I'd encountered on the street walked in. She started, a bit unsteadily, toward the bar, saw me, and changed her direction. She took a chair at a table about twelve feet from ours, signaled to Steve behind the bar, and then fixed her red-brown eyes on me.

Quickly I shifted my own gaze from her to Bill, and tried to concentrate on his words. He was talking about the male sea horse, who carries eggs around in a pouch until the young hatch out. It was interest-ing, and I wanted to listen. But every time that, in spite of myself, I glanced to my left, she was still sitting there, with what looked like a double bourbon in her hand, and her eyes fixed broodingly on me. I lost the thread of Bill's talk, found it, lost it again—

"Hey!" he said. "Looks as if we're ready for a refill."

"No, thank you. In fact, maybe we'd better—"

A chair scraped over the floor. Perhaps she'd seen me reach for my purse and gloves. Anyway, she was moving toward us, glass in hand, with a purposeful air. Looking surprised, Bill got to his feet.

She said, "Hello, Bill. You don't have to introduce Miss Warren. I know who she is." Then, to me: "I'm Mary Manwell. You mind if I join you?"

I said, trapped, "No. But we were just about to—"

"This won't take long." She jerked a chair back from the table, sat. "What did the Crandall girl tell you about me?"

"She never mentioned you. In fact"— and how tired I was of explaining that!— "she never said much about anything or anyone."

"Then I'll tell you about me! I've worked hard, understand? I spent the best years of

96

my life as a nurse. Not one of your high-paid R.N.'s in a fancy hospital, oh, no! I was a practical nurse. Riding herd on drunks with d.t.'s in one of those drying-out sanitariums. Carrying trays and emptying bedpans for old people in a god-awful nursing home."

She took a swallow of her drink, and then went on, "When my mother left me her house and four acres up here, I took some of the money I'd saved and opened my animal shelter. Why? Because I love animals! I love them just as much as that Crandall brat ever did."

"Miss Manwell, it seems to me—"

"Maybe I didn't keep up the place as well as I wanted to. I couldn't afford it. People were mighty stingy with their contributions. But I did the best I could. There was no reason why that Crandall—"

"Miss Manwell, all that happened quite awhile ago. Anyway, Laurabelle's dead now."

Her voice rose. "Does that help me? My shelter's been closed down. I may have to go back to nursing—if I can get a job," she said broodingly. "Those stories that I neglected those poor beasts won't help me get a job, not one little bit—"

Bill said, "Maybe you shouldn't talk about it any more tonight."

"Don't you tell me when to stop talking! I'm old enough to be your mother. I should have sued for slander," she said, still in that brooding voice. "Maybe I will sue—"

A man in khaki shirt and trousers had come into the bar. He was bald and short, with a heavy midsection that strained his shirt buttons. I saw his eyes, small gray ones, look swiftly around the room, and then rest on us. He walked over to our table.

"*Some*body ought to pay for what she did to me." Mary Manwell was saying. "You spend the best years of your life—"

"Now, Mary!" The stout man rested his hand on her shoulder. "You're not going to act up, are you? If you do, I'll have to run you in." He laughed to show he didn't mean it. "Hello, Bill. Oh, sit down, sit down! You've been up here long enough to know we're just plain folks. We don't go for all that fancy popping up and down."

"Sorry, Chief," Bill said amiably.

"How'd you make out in New York? Finally find yourself a girl?"

Bill said, "I'm afraid you've lost me."

"Weren't you down there about the mid-

98

dle of last month? I was there for a Rifle Association meeting, and I thought sure I saw you coming out of Radio City Music Hall—alone."

"Must have been some other four-eyed fellow. I haven't been to New York for nearly a year. And the last time I went to the Music Hall it was to see *Random Harvest.* I was eight years old, and in love with Greer Garson."

The stout man said, with an air of tolerant disbelief, "Well, have it your way." From time to time he'd been glancing at me. Now he said, eyes on my face, "Well, Bill, aren't you going to introduce me to your lady friend?"

Some people have a way of looking at each new acquaintance with slyly cynical eyes, as if they guessed some shabby secret that the other person had hidden from the world. The stout man was practicing that form of one-upmanship now.

"Jane," Bill said, "this is Mort Jones. He's our Chief of Police here in Garth. This is Miss Warren, Chief."

"Oh, yes. The young lady who came up here to tell Adele Newcombe what happened to her niece."

I opened my mouth and then, feeling

hopeless, closed it.

"Well," he continued, "I think I'll buy all of you a drink. Hey, Steve! Bring everybody here what they're drinking. And I'll have a beer."

"Thank you," I said, "but we were just leaving."

"That's right," Bill said.

Chief Jones pulled out the fourth chair and sat down. "Now listen, you two," he said with jocular ferocity. "Don't you know it's a risky business, turning down the law when he offers you a drink? That's right, isn't it, Mary?"

She'd fallen into gloomy silence. Eyes fixed on the tray-laden Steve who moved toward us, she merely shrugged. As the drinks were set on the table, Bill sent me an inquiring look, and I answered with my eyes, "It's all right."

"Here's how," Chief Jones said, hoisting his glass beer mug. He drank, and then looked at me. "I hear you're some kind of writer."

"Not really. It's my drawings I get by on."

"An artist, huh. We've got some artists living up here. And a lot more come in the summertime. From New York, mainly. All kinds of New Yorkers come up here, and I mean *all* kinds. Real swingers, some of them."

None of us said anything to that. After a moment he went on, "It must be pretty dull for a New York girl up here on the Cape this time of year. No swinging parties." He seemed to be hung up on swingers and swinging. "None of those spicy foreign movies you get down in New York—"

That irritated me. With no idea that I'd soon regret saying it, I answered, "Oh, I brought a supply of pot with me. When I get too bored, I'll just light up." Then I smiled as pleasantly as I could. "I was joking, of course. I love it here. In fact, maybe I'm a throwback. My mother's people lived on the Cape, five or six generations ago."

Soon after that, we thanked Chief Jones for the drinks and said good night. Mary Manwell, feeding a dime into the juke box, responded to our farewells with a gloomy nod.

As Bill's somewhat shabby but still rakish Jaguar moved down Main Street, he said, "I hope Mary Manwell didn't spoil your evening."

"Of course not. I feel sorry for her.

Maybe she did do the best she could with her animal shelter."

"Maybe." He paused. "How do you like our Chief of Police?"

"Remind me not to get myself arrested while I'm up here."

Bill chuckled, and then said, "Oh, hell. I wish I didn't have to fly down to New Jersey tomorrow."

We rode the rest of the way in a companionable silence, broken only by bossa nova music from the car radio. When we'd stopped beside my little rented house, he drew me into his arms and kissed me.

Releasing me, he said, "I don't suppose you'd ask me in for a nightcap."

"I wouldn't mind, but my dog's an awful prude."

He laughed. "Well, I figured there was no harm in trying. I'll see you to your door, anyway."

We climbed the stairs, and I unlocked the door. "Good night, and thank you for a highly interesting evening."

"Next time we'll do some of the bars farther down the Cape. Well, see you in about two weeks."

He'd started down the steps when I said, "Bill."

He turned. "Yes?"

"Several times this evening I meant to ask you, but something else always came up. Did you know Laura?"

"You mean the Crandall girl? She left here only a few weeks after I arrived on the Cape. I hardly knew her."

Eight

The weather held for the next three days. Reluctant to stay indoors, I'd work for an hour or two at my sketching board or typewriter, and then take off in the Volkswagen. I crossed the Cape to the high ramparts of Nauset Beach and stood watching the giant Atlantic rollers smash against their base, each wave bringing an infinitesimal bit closer the day when the waters will swirl over the last crumbling remnants of those cliffs. I drove up the Cape to the vast area of dunes, some of them tall as a three-story building, near Provincetown, and saw that Bill had been right. They did look like a Late Show movie with a North African setting. I almost expected to see David Niven, in Foreign Legion kepi and baggy trousers, come striding over the brow of the next dune.

After seeing that miniature Sahara, I found it hard to believe the statement in my guidebook, bought at the drugstore in Garth, that only a few miles away I'd find a moss-hung swamp reminiscent of Louisiana. But it was true. Later that afternoon I moved on foot down a trail through a thickening wood of oak and pitch pine. The undergrowth became more dense, and the canopy of interlacing branches heavier, shutting out the sun. And then suddenly there it was, a grove of cedar trees standing in perpetual twilight, a gray moss hanging from their boughs, their roots in black, spreading water. There was no sound— none at all. I turned and moved rapidly up the path, eager to return to my rented house beside the bay.

Because it was the less spectacular wonders of "my" beach that delighted me most. The dune grass beside my little house, with sunlight running like molten silver along its gracefully bent blades. The skittering sandpipers, and the perpetually squabbling herring gulls, and the magnificent, almost fearless black-backed gulls, who'd let me approach within a few feet before they rose, great wings beating the air with a down-thrust so powerful I felt it in my own body. I collected driftwood specimens by the armful, even though I realized I couldn't take all of it back to New York with me. And once I found a bit of gray shale which—perhaps thousands or even millions of years ago—had received and retained the delicate impress of a bird's foot.

I continued to have dinner on the beach —more elaborate ones, with salad and fruit compote carried down to the sand in glass jars. After I'd taken Howie up to his pallet —he still considered a nighttime beach no fit place for a dog—I'd return to the sand. With the aid of a flashlight and a paper-backed copy of *Astronomy for Beginners*, also purchased at the Garth drugstore, I'd pick out the constellations swarming overhead— the Swan, which that first night had looked to me like a jet plane, and the Lyre, whose chief star, blue-white Vega, I'd also noticed that first evening, and my own birth sign, Sagittarius.

When tired of star-gazing, I'd take a stroll along the water's edge. The first night I did so I discovered to my delight that each step scattered sparks over the damp sand. They were, I suppose, some sort of tiny phosphorescent creatures. But I felt like some mythical goddess, awakening fire from the earth wherever she trod.

Sunburned, drowsy, and growing a bit chilled, I'd return to my dying fire and gather up my dinner paraphernalia. Feeling, if not happy, then at least extraordinarily content, I'd climb the steps.

Gabe Harmon appeared on each of those first three full days I spent in the little house. The first morning, just as I was getting out my sketch board, he drove up in a Ford station wagon. When he was halfway up the steps, I came out onto the sun deck.

He'd found a pair of sun glasses in that bathroom on the hotel's second floor, he said. Had I left them?

I hadn't.

"Well, see you," he said, and turned away.

Late the next afternoon he was there again. Luke Carberry, he told me, had said last summer's tenants had complained of a loose gas connection on the kitchen range. Had I had any trouble with it?

"No, no trouble."

"Well, I'd better get back to the hotel."

When he'd gone, I reflected that he could have found out about both the sun glasses and the stove by merely picking up the phone. Why these visits? Was he checking up on me, for some reason or another? Could it be that he still suspected I'd lied about my reason for coming here?

Then I gave myself a vigorous mental shake. Surely, just because of that so-and-so Kevin, I wasn't going to become one of those dreary, self-deprecating females. Why not assume that he made those unnecessary visits because he found me attractive? True, on both occasions his manner had been almost as laconic and deadpan as on the night I arrived at his hotel. But still—

When he knocked on the door the next evening, I was preparing coffee to take down to the sand. I said, as he walked past me into the living room, "Care to join me for a beach dinner? I've got an extra lamb chop."

Turning, he stared at me. "A beach dinner? In early April?"

"Why not? We big city people are tough. Have to be, to hold up under all that coal smoke and exhaust fumes."

"Well, thanks. I can't right now. But I came to ask you about Saturday night. Down the Cape there's a good restaurant that stays open all year. Would you have dinner with me?"

"Why, I'd like to very much." Instantly I hoped I hadn't sounded too pleased.

"Fine. I'll pick you up at six." He started toward the door, and then turned back. "I hear you were at the tavern the other night with Bill Brockton."

"Yes. He's very nice."

"He seems okay." To my secret pleasure, his tone was a bit grudging. "Everyone says he's quite a brain—already in the National Academy of Science, and all that. Well, see you Saturday."

He left, and I returned, smiling, to the kitchen. First Bill, who was interesting and nice, even if he didn't exactly turn me on. And now Gabe, who perhaps wasn't as nice—I couldn't be sure yet—but who definitely, in my book, was a turner-on.

With an inward giggle, I thought, "Maybe I shouldn't let word get around." If New York girls learned about the off-season supply of men in summer resorts, entire stenographic pools would be demanding March vacations.

The next day was even warmer than the previous ones, but thin cirrus clouds, now and then dimming the sunlight, hinted at coming rain. Eager to enjoy the good weather while it lasted, I worked for less than an hour, then changed to a sweater and shorts and knee-high socks, and carried *Quo Vadis?* with me down to the beach. I spent the rest of the day reading, and walking down the beach to admire the amber and purple kelp brought in by the last tide, and just lying in the sun.

By five-thirty the windless air still felt warm, but distinctly heavy and damp. Determined to have at least one more beach dinner, I exchanged my shorts for heavy black cotton tights and a plaid wool skirt. After packing my cardboard box, I carried it to the sand and set off with Howie to search for kindling and for campfire wood. To my dismay, I saw that my previous dinners had made serious inroads on the supply of driftwood. We'd walked about half a mile before I collected a sufficient amount.

Consequently, by the time I'd eaten lamb chops and salad and was ready for coffee, the dark had already thickened, those homeless creatures in the swamp had uttered their first yelps, and Howie had begun to crowd close to me and whimper. I took him up to the house. Returning to the sand, I drank my coffee and then piled driftwood on the glowing charcoal.

I don't know how much later it was that I became aware of feeling dizzy. Perhaps I'd overstrained my eyes, reading in alternate sun and shadow on the beach that day, and now staring at the fire for— How long had I been staring at that dancing brightness? It seemed like hours, and yet it couldn't be, because the flames were still shooting high, and I hadn't piled on more driftwood. At least I couldn't remember doing so.

There was something wrong with the fire itself. On other nights I'd seen little flames of green or cobalt blue lick the salt-laden wood, but I'd never seen blood-red flames. They were in the fire now, though, curving around the thicker end of a long-dead tree branch and then, when I looked at the other end, springing up there. More than salt in that wood. It must have been soaked in some other chemical.

Don't look at it. Rest your eyes. Lie back and look up at the sky.

I was on my back now, although I didn't remember moving. Just above the shooting flames and smoke, there seemed to be a sullen, yellowish patch on the night sky. But beyond that patch the dome overhead was black, black, and infinitely far away.

A wide streak of blood-red light shot

across the black heavens.

A meteor? No, it couldn't be. Meteor paths were much thinner, and more orange than red.

Aware of cold sand grating under the back of my head, I turned my face toward the black, dully shining bay. About where the horizon should be, a streak of blood-red shot across the blackness.

I thought, with confused terror, "What's gone wrong?" Had it come, the Armageddon the world had been expecting for so many years? No, there was no sudden, terrible brightness, lighting up beach and sea and sky for one last split second. The earth beneath me did not dissolve.

Then it was worse. There'd been some grotesque alteration in the very nature of the universe.

Or in me.

No! You do not go insane, all in an instant, with no warning. You do not take your dog up to his pallet, and come back to your campfire and go insane. You just don't.

Talk to someone. Bill. He was a scientist. He'd know what— But he was gone. Gabe, then. Get to the phone.

I rose to my feet in what seemed to me

just one smooth motion. And then, through my bewilderment and fear, another emotion began to swell, an exuberant sense of power. I felt that, if I chose, I could leap as high as those flames leapt. A moment later that crazy exultance faded, leaving me more terrified than before. So it was something in me that had gone wrong. I sank to the sand.

A girl was whimpering. It was Jane Warren. I saw her sitting there, arms crossed over her chest, and whimpering.

Quite suddenly, I was back in my body, and fighting for breath. Something rough and opaque had come down over my head, my shoulders, my arms. It blotted out the soaring fire. Except, of course, for the blood-red flames. They kept leaping in the blackness.

Nine

For an interval—I cannot say how long—I sat paralyzed, unable to struggle against the enshrouding roughness. And when I did try, it was too late. Something had been wound tight around my waist and whatever enveloped me, binding my arms to my sides.

I was standing up. Had something, someone, raised me to my feet? Perhaps so, because now, while the flames still licked in the half-smothering blackness, I was being propelled, stumbling, over ground that sloped upward.

Rasp of metal, almost painfully loud. Hands pushing, lifting, until I sat on something smooth. Smell of leather. I was inside a car.

Metallic slam of a door on my right. Then, after what seemed a long time, that painful rasping sound as the other door opened, slammed shut. An engine caught, with deafening loudness.

A turning motion made me sway helplessly toward the right-hand corner of the seat. Then we moved forward over a surface that dipped, rose, dipped. I was on a roller coaster, tearing through the flame-shot dark. And if I liked, with one small effort I could break whatever bound me.

I tried, and the bonds held.

For a lucid second I thought, "A drug. The coffee. Who—"

I heard myself speaking aloud. "Who? What?"

No answer. Just motion along a surface that had smoothed out. That, and the flame-shot blackness, shutting out air. But not entirely. In fact, as the flames dimmed, I could see a pattern of darkness and light—headlights bathing the road ahead?—like a miniature checkerboard.

Burlap over my head? A burlap bag?

Then the red flames thickened again, and the roller coaster dipped and rose, and exultance flooded me. A shout gathered in my chest and throat.

Deep within me a self-preserving some-thing counseled, "Don't bottle it up. Let it out." Just as the roller coaster carried my body, I must allow whatever had seized my mind to sweep me along. If I fought it, it would destroy me utterly. I shouted, and swayed against a shoulder. A hand, not roughly, pushed me toward the other cor-ner of the seat.

For an unmeasured time I traveled, some-times by car, sometimes by roller coaster, through what I knew was an endless picture gallery in my mind. The little flames had given way to flowers, which bloomed and swelled like elaborate fireworks, and to faces. All of them, whether friendly or menacing, looked familiar, but to none of them could I attach a name and anyway, almost at once, each of them melted into another face.

From the edge of the road along which the car traveled, laughter struck painfully at my ears. It was a two-note laugh, rising and then falling. While that laughter still sounded, we made another turn, and I swayed so far to one side that I nearly fell out of the roller coaster and plunged down through miles of darkness.

Another turn, and a long plunge. A hollow thunder below us, as if we moved across a giant kettledrum. Rising ground. And then suddenly no sound, and no motion, except that of a purple and orange pinwheel, whirling in the blackness.

A metal door rasped open, slammed closed. Another rasp, and cold wetness blew against my legs. "Get out." A breathy quality to the words. They'd been whispered. And yet to my ears they'd sounded loud.

Hands, drawing me off the leather seat. An arm around me, pulling me through something—weeds?—tall grass?—that whipped against my legs. Wetness pounding on the cloth that enveloped me, and soaking through to my hair. For a moment or two my brain seemed to clear. Rain. The rain had started.

Again that whisper. "Step up." Something solid underfoot now. I heard the grate of metal against metal, the rattle of a chain, and then the complaint of door hinges. The arm propelled me forward, caught me as I stumbled. Again a voice whispered, "Step up!" I obeyed, and the arm dropped from around me. A musty smell now. Rain no longer beat down upon my head, but I could hear its thunderous pound upon something high above me.

Another rasping sound, so unpleasant that I flinched, and then a whiff of sulfur mingling with that musty smell. A match. Someone had struck a match.

Hands on my shoulders, pressing down. "Sit." Then rope was tightening around my ankles. "My legs are being tied to a chair's legs," I thought, and, incongruously, felt a vast relief. At least I knew it was a chair, and not the seat of a roller coaster. And the chair was in a room, with the rain drumming on its roof.

Whatever bound my waist loosened slightly. Then hands reached under the enshrouding cloth, grasped my hands, and pulled them backward. Something thin—cord? fishing line?—bit into my crossed wrists. Quite suddenly, the smothering darkness lifted from me, and I blinked in the light of a candle, a fat yellow candle. Stuck in the mouth of a glass jug, it had been placed on a small rough table, so close to where I sat that I could feel the flame's wavering warmth. Fascinated, I stared at it, and as I did so the flame shot high, with streaks of green and blue and red spiraling through it.

Footsteps. Someone moved past me, past

the table. Candlelight flickered over a wet black raincoat. It was topped by a rain-soaked hat that seemed grotesquely incongruous with the black slicker. It was the sort of white, floppy-brimmed hat that men and women and children wear at the beach in midsummer. I tried to keep sight of that figure, but the dazzle of candlelight made a screen before my eyes.

Now I could see someone, over there by those tiny windowpanes, each of which reflected the flame of the candle. It was a black, short shape, topped with a white blur— Short? The raincoated figure that had passed the table had been tall. He must be sitting down now. Yes, that was it.

"Why did you come to Garth?" The breathy voice carried distinctly to my ears.

"Kevin. He threw me over. I wanted to go away from New York." Dimly I was aware that to others I hadn't spoken of Kevin. But now, somehow, it was impossible to speak anything but the full truth.

"But why Garth, particularly? It was because you knew Laurabelle came from here, wasn't it?"

"No. I didn't know where she came from."

"What did she tell you about Mary Field?"

"I don't know anyone named Mary Field."

A long pause. "I didn't ask you that. What did Laurabelle tell you about Mary Field?"

"She didn't. She never mentioned her."

Another pause. I stared at the candle. Little blood-red flames like tiny, licking tongues. I didn't like them. There. They'd gone.

"You know who killed Laurabelle, don't you?"

"Yes. A hit-and-run driver."

"But what was the driver's name?"

I peered through the screening dazzle at that dim figure. Could it be Satan? It seemed to dwindle, and then to swell, blackly, and I cried, in sudden revulsion and terror, "It was you. You killed her and left her lying in the street."

After a long while the breathy voice asked, "And who am I?" Incredibly, I detected a note of fear. Could the devil be afraid?

"I don't know who you are. Maybe someone in my brain."

All at once my fear had dimmed, giving

way to a cold, grinding depression. Whether this was reality or nightmare or madness, I was trapped in it, as if in hell. I'd sit here forever, with the drum of rain in my ears, and my eyes peering through the screen of wavering light at that black, somehow obscene figure over there beside the tiny, candle-reflecting panes.

"She phoned you the night she was killed."

"Yes." I was becoming so very tired. If I could just close my eyes against the candle-light, and sink forever into sleep, as if into black, obliterating water.

"She was afraid of someone. Whose name did she give you?"

It was an effort to speak. "She gave no name. She just said something had happened, and she wanted to come to my place."

"Tell me again why you came to Garth."

This *was* hell. Those medieval paintings which showed damned souls set to endless, useless tasks, such as ladling wine into a vat with a gushing hole in its side. This was the senseless task to which I'd been doomed, answering these questions over and over again.

"Kevin. He's going to marry someone

else. I wanted to get away from New York."

"Keep your eyes open. But you also knew Laurabelle came from Garth."

Impossible to keep my eyelids from drooping. "No, I didn't know." I let my eyes close and my head fall forward. Mercifully, the voice across the room didn't speak.

A fumbling at whatever bound my wrists. My right hand, falling free, caught momentarily on something sharp, but I was only dimly aware of pain. The half-smothering shroud came down over my head, and someone wrapped rope around me, binding my unresisting arms to my sides. My ankles were released.

"Get up."

Stumbling, more unconscious than not, I felt myself propelled forward.

Ten

Eyes still closed, I awoke to dampness, to the grit of wet sand under my left cheek, and, upon my right, a patter of light, cold rain.

I raised eyelids that felt swollen, and stared at the blackened embers of my campfire. Beyond them, the empty beach stretched for perhaps fifty yards, before it was dimmed and then swallowed up by the misty drizzle.

Dazed and unbelieving, I lay for perhaps a minute in the same position in which I'd awakened, knees slightly drawn up, each hand resting on the opposite shoulder. How could I have fallen asleep down here and, what was more inexplicable, slept all night despite a heavy rain? Because it had been heavy. The wet beach was now dark brown rather than beige, and my soaked skirt and sweater weighed grittily upon my body.

Aching, I sat up and looked out over the gray, dully shining water. I couldn't see far. A wall of white mist hid the horizon. What time was it? Well past dawn, certainly. Even in the foggy drizzle, some quality of the light told me that. I looked at my watch and saw that it had stopped at five minutes of two.

But that was not what kept me staring downward, gaze riveted. It was the long splinter, blunt end protruding slightly from beneath the skin, which had lodged itself in the back of my hand. I had a swift memory of my limp hand, briefly impaling itself on something sharp and then falling free. Swiftly I pushed up one sweater sleeve, then the other. Each wrist was braceleted with a pink indentation.

The whole nightmare came back to me then. Blood-red streaks splitting a black sky. The roller coaster ride through the picture gallery of blooming flowers and dissolving faces. The dim shape in the black raincoat and absurd, floppy hat, asking questions about Laura.

Nightmare? I stared at the splinter ridging the cold-reddened back of my hand. Nightmare?

Up in the beach house, Howie gave one bark. It sounded feeble and despairing, as if he'd been barking all night.

Stiff and aching, I got to my feet. As I turned toward the house, I stumbled over the sodden cardboard box in which I'd packed my dinner paraphernalia, and fell to my hands and knees. I didn't bother with the box, nor with the rumpled, sodden blanket that lay near it. Getting to my feet, I staggered through the heavy wet sand and, grasping the handrail, pulled myself up the steps.

Puppyish in his hysterical relief, Howie hurled his aged bulk upon me as soon as I opened the door, so that I had to clutch the jamb to keep from falling. Nausea hit me at the same time, making the room swim around me. As fast as I could, lest the black mist close in on me before I reached it, I staggered to the bedroom and fell face down on the bed.

The springs gave as Howie hoisted himself up beside me. Ordinarily that was forbidden, but now his rough-coated presence was a comfort. One hand resting on his head, I waited until the nausea passed, waited until a spark of anger began to glow beneath my fear and bewilderment.

Someone had drugged and kidnaped me. And I was going to do something about it.

Turning my head, I looked at my little traveling clock on the bedside stand. Almost seven. By eight, Chief Jones might be in his office.

Still faintly nauseated, but no longer dizzy, I went into the small bathroom and setting my teeth, pulled the heavy splinter free with a pair of tweezers. The wound bled slightly. I daubed it with iodine and placed a ready-made adhesive bandage over it. Then I turned steaming water into the tub and stripped my sodden clothes from me.

Even after the hot bath, even after I'd dressed in my best wool suit, I felt dizzy and disoriented, but at the same time my tonic anger had grown. At the bathroom mirror I stared at my reflection—slightly unfamiliar with its pallor beneath the faint tan, its oddly contracted pupils—and then put on lipstick.

The drug, I realized, must have been placed in my thermos of coffee. And anyone could have done it. Almost literally, anyone. Our driftwood foraging had carried

Howie and me far up the beach. Anyone could have come down to that cardboard box and slipped something into the thermos.

Slipped what? Sodium pentothal? Could that be taken orally? Certainly amphetamines and LSD could. Perhaps it had been a combination of drugs. Well, the police could find out. I'd take the thermos with me. Surely it would hold traces of the drug.

Hurrying now, I opened my purse to make sure my car keys were in it. "Yes," I said to Howie, who was whining, his eyes quite yellow with anxiety. "I'm going away again, but I'll be back soon."

Going down the stairs, I crossed the heavy damp sand to the limp cardboard box. Stooping, I rummaged among the grate, the cooking fork, the sodden bag of unused charcoal, and the lamb chop bone, wrapped in paper now soaked and torn, which I'd planned to give to Howie. The thermos wasn't there.

Straightening, I stared down at the box. In my righteous rage, I'd thought that I had only to go to the police to have my abductor brought, eventually, to book. But now I felt a chill premonition. Without that thermos—

The splinter wound in my hand. The rope marks around my wrists. Those would be enough to lend credence. Of course they would. I moved up to the Volkswagen.

Before opening its door, I turned and stared at the reedy marsh stretching between the dunes and the dark pine woods, showing dimly through the misty rain that hid Joshua's Swamp. Could he have tossed the thermos there, among the tall reeds? No, he wouldn't have been so foolish as to dispose of it that nearby. The thermos could be almost anywhere. Tossed into woods miles from here. Weighted with stones and sunk in one of the Cape's many ponds. Reposing on some village dump.

Then, with a momentary lifting of my spirits, I noticed the deep ruts dug into the clayey soil just behind the VW. A much heavier car than my own little bug had made those ruts. Then I realized that they could have been made by any of numerous cars, and not necessarily last night. Perhaps Luke Carberry's Chrysler had made them, or Gabe's Ford station wagon, or Bill Brockton's Jaguar, or the delivery truck which, two afternoons ago, had brought a new cylinder of butane gas for the stove. Sometimes in the late afternoon fishermen had driven up to wade far out onto the tidal flats, and twice in the small hours I'd been awakened by the sound of departing cars which, probably, had held lovers.

And anyway, the ruts were filled with rain water. There'd probably be no chance of learning what particular set of tires had made them, let alone when.

Quickly, trying to stave off a leaden depression that was like something I'd felt not long ago—oh, yes, in that room, with the black figure beyond the veil of candlelight—I jerked open the Volkswagen's door.

Eleven

I found Garth already astir. On the hotel veranda, Mr. Dudley wielded a push broom. He didn't look up as I passed. A group of book-laden teen-agers stood on the corner in front of the pharmacy, evidently waiting for a school bus. A steel gate still barred the entrance to the bank, but Howard Simpson was unlocking the door of his grocery store. A vaguely familiar blond woman passed me, driving an old sedan, and after a moment I realized she was the hairdresser, Miss Carruthers.

The double doors of Town Hall stood open. I parked outside, and then walked down the broad hall. The door marked *Chief of Police* was the second one to the left, just beyond the Town Clerk's.

In the outer office, a lanky, freckled young man sat at a desk. He was typing by the hunt-and-peck system, a concentrated frown furrowing his forehead. He looked up. After a moment he asked, "You want something, miss?"

"Is the Chief of Police in?"

"Sure. You go right through there."

I opened the inner door. Chief Jones said, head bent over an opened desk drawer, "Carl, where the hell is—"

He looked up, closed the drawer, and said, "Well, if it isn't Miss Warren." He leaned back in his swivel chair. "Have a seat." Then, when I'd sat down in the chair on the other side of the desk: "Now what can I do for you?"

Clutching my handbag in my lap, I remained silent for several seconds. Until now, when he'd fixed those cynical little eyes on my face, I hadn't realized how absurd I was going to sound.

"What is it? Somebody break into your car?"

I blurted, "Last night someone drugged and kidnaped me."

For a moment there was silence. Then his chair creaked as he leaned forward. "Go on."

"I'd just finished my dinner down on the beach when—"

"You had dinner on the beach? In April, in the *rain?*"

"The rain hadn't started yet. It wasn't too cold, and I was warmly dressed."

"Who was with you?"

"No one."

"A girl has a cookout on the beach all by herself?"

With an irritability I instantly regretted, I said, "Yes! Maybe it seems to you unusual, but it's no crime. And if you keep interrupting me—"

Although he smiled, his eyes had grown cold. "Keep talking. I won't say a word."

"It was after I finished my coffee. I—I think the drug had been put in the coffee. If I had the thermos, maybe—but it's gone. Anyway, I began to feel strange—"

With those little eyes never leaving my face, I stumbled on. Perhaps if his gaze hadn't disconcerted me so, I'd have gone into less detail. But, afraid that under that steady stare I'd lose the thread of my account, I told him everything I could remember—the red streaks across the sky, the harsh laughter I'd heard at the roadside just before the car made a turn, even the

132

dreadful, grinding depression I'd felt in that strange room.

"I woke up on the beach in front of my house. And when I looked for the thermos, it wasn't in the box. I came here and—that's all."

He stared at me for a long moment and then, smiling, leaned back in his swivel chair. "That was quite a trip you had. Quite—a—trip."

As I looked back at him, uncertain of his meaning, he asked, "How many times you taken LSD, Miss Warren?"

After a long moment I managed to say, "You think I—why, I've never—"

"Look, Miss Warren, I may be just a village cop, but village cops can read. I know what that stuff does."

"You think I deliberately—"

"Aw, come on, Janey. You don't mind if I call you Janey, do you? You've already admitted you smoke marijuana."

"I didn't admit it! I *said* I did. It was a joke. You must have known it was a joke. If I really smoke marijuana, would I say so? To you?"

"Oh, I don't know. Seems to me kids these days like to flaunt that sort of thing."

My nerves snapped. "I'm not a kid. I'm twenty-four. And I've been the victim of a criminal act. Are you going to do something about it, or aren't you?"

The round face froze. After a moment he reached into a drawer and then placed a sheet of paper on his desk. Ballpoint pen poised, he asked in a coldly businesslike voice, "Who was the man?"

"I've already told you. I have no idea! I'm not even sure it was a man." Those breathy words, so distinct to my drug-sharpened hearing, could possibly have been those of a contralto-voiced woman.

He said aloud, busily writing, "Complainant doesn't know sex of her assailant." He looked up. "Was the person tall?"

"Yes." Then: "I'm not sure." I recalled how everything—the candleflame, the flowers and faces that swam across my vision, the black-coated figure across the room—seemed to change shape and size.

Again he wrote. "Now where was this house he took you to?"

"I don't know. I told you. There was something over my head. A burlap bag, I think."

Pokerfaced now, he made another notation. "Well, how far away was it from the house you've rented?"

My voice sounded flat. "I don't know." Between the moment I last looked at my weirdly altered campfire and the moment I first blinked in the light of the candle, hours might have passed, or only minutes. I added, anticipating him, "And I have no idea what direction we took."

He dropped the pen and sat back. "You want an investigation, and you can't give me a thing to go on, not a thing."

"I've told all that happened!" With sudden inspiration, I said, "I told you that he questioned me about someone named Mary Field. That's something to go on."

"Not for me, it isn't. Nobody of that name around here. There's a Dave Field down near Eastham, but all his kids are boys. And his wife's name isn't Mary. It's Janice, Janet, something like that."

I leaned forward. "You've got to find him. What he did to me was bad enough. But don't you understand? He killed Laura."

He said, pretending puzzlement, "Laura?"

"You know who I mean!" I wanted to

135

cry. "Laurabelle, Laurabelle Crandall."

"Oh. Laurabelle. Now look. You were the one who came up here and said she died in an accident. Hit-and-run. And now you—"

"The police said that was how she died." I was beginning to feel very tired. "They must have told Mrs. Newcombe that by now. Hasn't she been in touch with them?"

"Yes. They still haven't found the driver. When all the red tape's unwound, she'll have Laurabelle's body brought here to Garth. Now, as near as I can make out, you've decided it was deliberate hit-and-run. Murder, in other words."

"I told you," I said wearily. Or had I? I was so tired, and Chief Jones kept looking at me with those sardonic little eyes—"I said to the—to the person, 'You killed her, didn't you?' and he didn't deny it."

"What did he say, exactly?"

"He said, 'Who am I?' "

"And?"

"I said, 'I don't know. Maybe—' " I broke off.

"Maybe?"

Oh, what was the use? "I told him that maybe he was someone in my brain."

Chief Jones smiled. "And maybe he was, maybe he was. And all the rest of it, too."

"No." I shook my head. "No. There was a splinter in my hand." I held out the hand with the bandage. "The splinter came off the chair in that house. I took it out, but it was there." I pushed up one jacket sleeve, then the other. The circular indentations were less pronounced now, but still visible. "Look at my wrists. The cord, or whatever it was, made those marks."

"Now, look. You could have got a splinter in your hand—if you really did—a dozen different ways. And those marks on your wrists, well—now don't get sore. I'm looking at it the way a policeman has to. You could have tied something around your own wrists."

I made one last try. "I saw ruts in the road behind my car this morning. Some other car had made them; some heavy car."

"Say!" With an enthusiastic expression, he leaned forward. "Now we're getting somewhere. I'll go right out and make a cast of those ruts. You can tell a lot from nice, dry tire prints."

How he must hate me. No, it couldn't be anything personal. It was just that it must be hard for him to keep that sadistic streak under control most of the time, lest he alienate those who'd put him in office. When he could safely let it out, he did so.

I said, "The ruts are filled with rain water. You know that."

"Then they aren't going to help us much, are they? Look. I've got an idea. You think Laurabelle was murdered. That's New York's case, not mine. You call the New York police and tell them what you've told me. Why, I bet you they'll solve the whole thing in no time. I've seen them on those TV crime shows. In an hour, even with time out for commercials, they can wrap up a whole case." He snapped his fingers. "Just like that."

As I shoved back my chair, he added, "Or why don't you just go home and go to bed for a while? Maybe when you wake up you'll decide it never happened. And when you go back to New York, maybe you'd better see one of those fancy doctors. People like you, artists and so on, you're all high-strung."

He didn't mean high-strung.

I left. In the outer office the lanky man stared at me with such frank wonderment that I knew he must have heard my conversation with Chief Jones, or at least part of it.

The drizzle had stopped, and the hovering mist was no longer gray and dull, but had a pearly luminescence, as if the sun were trying to struggle through. As I drove beyond Garth, and then turned left off the highway onto the narrower side road, I wondered if I could be, in Chief Jones's euphemism, high-strung. I'd always regarded myself as healthy. But could insanity strike all at once, like those white squalls I'd read about, those squalls which come out of nowhere on a cloudless day and then subside, leaving only wreckage to testify to their demonic force? No, I told myself emphatically. There'd been the splinter in my hand, and the rope marks on my wrists, no matter how airily Chief Jones had tried to dismiss them. Above all, there was the thermos bottle, or rather, its absence. That alone was enough to assure me that last night's experience had been real.

Leaving the car parked between the dunes, I crossed the damp sand and started up the wooden stairs. Then I halted. Something down there on the sand, visible through the space between two plank steps, had caught my eye. Something tan in color. All thought suspended, I descended the planks and walked under the staircase.

It was the thermos. Almost upright, it leaned against one side of a hollow in the sand. Rain water filled it to the brim. Perhaps a foot away lay its tan plastic cap, coated with sand. Had it been there when I climbed these stairs early this morning? In all probability, yes. Dizzy and weak, I hadn't looked down as I climbed, but kept my eye on the door behind which Howie scrambled.

For a moment more I stared at it leaning there where it might have landed if someone had dropped it on the stairs and then inadvertently struck it with his foot. Had I dropped it? While in hallucination I'd ridden a car-roller coaster through a night filled with clashing colors, and sat bound in a room with many-paned windows, had I in reality never left this beach? Had I wandered, witless, up and down these stairs, and finally fallen into a stupor beside the blackened remains of my campfire?

I reached up and caught one of the planks to steady myself. "Oh, please," I whispered, "oh, please." Let it be true, the room, the man in the black slicker, all of it. The alternative was so much more frightening.

Don't think about it now, I commanded myself. Rest first, rest. Leaving the thermos down there in the sand, I climbed the stairs, entered my house, and followed Chief Jones's advice. I went to bed.

Twelve

My exhaustion must have been greater than I'd realized, because I actually slept. When I awoke, a little after two in the afternoon, the bedroom window framed watery, pale blue sky. The rain seemed to be over.

So was my self-doubt. As I dressed in my good plaid suit—no beach dinner tonight; no more beach dinners ever, not here—I found I felt infinitely better.

It had really happened. That splinter proved it, and the marks on my wrists. They'd faded now, but they'd been there. As for the thermos, my abductor had placed it there.

It seemed to me that there'd been a quite lengthy interval between the time I'd been thrust into the car and the time I'd heard the door open on the driver's side. I pictured him hurrying back to the sand, wading out to rinse the thermos and its cap in sea water, and then placing it, almost upright, under the stairs, so that it would catch the imminent rain. True, he could have put it back where I'd packed it away, under the folded canvas. But then its complete absence of coffee traces inside, and of my fingerprints outside, would have appeared significant. Standing at the living room window, looking out over water a shade darker than the pale blue sky, I felt a return of the bracing fury that had filled me that morning.

What should I do now? Go back to New York? That's what my abductor was expecting me to do, cut and run. My abductor, who'd also killed my friend, murdered her in a more cowardly fashion, but just as surely as if he'd put a gun to her head.

I'd feel uneasy, staying here. But he would be no threat to me, at least for a while, simply because he thought I was no threat to him. He'd ransacked my mind, laid open to him by the drug, as thoroughly as he might have searched the drawers and pigeonholes of a desk. He was sure now that I hadn't known why Laura fled from

Garth, or even that she'd lived here. He knew that I had no idea who had struck her down in the street. What's more, he'd soon know—everyone would know—that I'd come to Chief Jones with a story he'd dismissed as the fantasy of a girl who was mentally unstable, or who had been turned on once too often.

Yes, I'd be expected to run back to New York now, and never tell that story again—except, perhaps, to the "fancy doctor" Chief Jones had mentioned. Again I felt a surge of rage.

But if I didn't run? Would that alarm the man who'd killed Laura? No, at least not immediately. He might well conclude that I'd become convinced there was something wrong with me, and that I was lingering on here, paralyzed with self-doubt, and afraid to rejoin my friends and associates in New York.

Quite suddenly, I became aware that I was hungry. After all, I'd had nothing to eat since the evening before. As I walked toward the kitchen I remembered that my supplies were low, and that, yesterday, I'd planned to shop in town today.

Supplies were even lower than I'd realized. Only two eggs in the small refrigerator, and no bacon. A third of a loaf of bread, an ounce or so of coffee, and only one can of dog food. I shrank from the idea of facing the townspeople. And yet I'd have to, and very soon, if I intended to stay here.

I percolated the last of the coffee, scrambled the eggs, and toasted bread slices in the antediluvian toaster—small, and of some dark metal—that had come with the place. I made out my grocery list. Then, with Howie in the back seat this time, I drove through the watery sunlight to Garth.

As I traveled, nerves braced, down Main Street, I saw Luke Carberry's gray Chrysler parked in front of the bank. A heavy car. Those deep ruts— But the ruts meant nothing. They could have been there, unnoticed by me, since before I'd moved into the house. Besides, whatever Laura had meant to him, even if she'd been the object of some thwarted, middle-aged passion, it was hard to imagine a politically ambitious man like Carberry deliberately running a girl down in the street. It was even harder to imagine him kidnaping a drugged girl to question her. For one thing, I doubted that he had either the brains to plan it, or the nerve to carry it through.

A thoroughly frightened man, though,

could transcend himself. A blackmailed man, for instance. Had Laura been blackmailing him, and had he feared, when I turned up in Garth, that she'd passed some dangerous knowledge on to me? Suddenly ashamed of myself, I remembered the lonely, haunted gray eyes, her pathetic enjoyment of our shared dinners, even those at the Automat, her wretched "light housekeeping room." Laura had been no blackmailer.

"Get your groceries," I told myself. Random speculation could only tire and confuse me. Later I'd go through my memories of last night methodically, like someone unpacking a trunk and examining each article.

The moment I walked up to the grocery store counter, I knew the story of my interview with Chief Jones had already spread over town. I knew it by the way both Mr. and Mrs. Simpson looked at the bandage on the back of my hand. I knew it by the faintly scandalized curiosity in the eyes they raised to my face.

I forced a smile. "Hello." Then, to Mr. Simpson: "I'd like some groceries. Here's the list."

He was placing canned goods on the

counter when a voice I recognized said, "Good afternoon, Mrs. Simpson. I'd like a package of that Ceylon tea of yours."

I turned. Mrs. Newcombe stood there in a well-cut tweed suit. Her dark head with that becoming silver streak was bare. One hand rested on a walking stick. Her gaze, too, went straight to the bandage on my hand. Then she looked up and said, "Good afternoon, Miss Warren."

"Good afternoon. I'm glad to see you're out and around."

"Thank you. But you don't look at all well, Miss Warren." Her eyes held a cold, amused shine as they rested on my face.

She'd lied to me about Laura that day, or at least she hadn't told me all the truth. I was sure of it. What's more, she was tall, and the hand grasping the walking stick looked broad and strong—

The walking stick. The woman had had a *stroke*, for heaven's sake! Why, to suspect her was simply—

I shied away from the word my thoughts had almost formed. As evenly as I could, I answered, "Well, perhaps I'm coming down with a cold."

"If you do, have Mr. Mathieson at the

drugstore mix you some of his cold capsules. They're good." She accepted a small paper bag. "That's the exact change, isn't it, Mrs. Simpson? Well, good-by, all."

Through the plate-glass window I watched her get behind the wheel of an old but well-polished Lincoln sedan. Her stroke must have been slight indeed, if she and Dr. Rainey thought it advisable for her to drive a car.

"That'll be eight-seventy," Mr. Simpson said. He took my ten-dollar bill, handed me change. "I'll carry this out to your car."

As he placed the box of groceries in the VW's trunk, I looked down the street. Mary Manwell, red hair bright in the feeble sunlight, was coming out of the pharmacy. She turned in the other direction.

Mary Manwell, brooding over the loss of her animal shelter, and the loss of the hard-earned savings she'd invested in it.

Mary Manwell. Mary Field.

"Stop it!" I told myself as I nodded good-by to Mr. Simpson. "Stop going at it hit-or-miss."

But of course I didn't stop. As I drove out of town and turned left onto the pine-bordered road that led toward the bay, I became conscious of a dull headache.

Nervous tension, or an aftereffect of the drug?

The drug. It had been some sort of hallucinogen, obviously, perhaps mixed with sodium pentothal. Who in town—besides Dr. Rainey, of course, and the pharmacist, whom I hadn't met—would have easy access to such drugs? Well, Mort Jones, in the course of his official duties, might have confiscated some LSD.

Come to think of it, I'd read somewhere that LSD was of such simple manufacture that a college freshman, with access to a chemical laboratory, could make it.

But who here in Garth would have both access to such equipment and the knowledge of how to use it?

There were laboratories at Woods Hole, no doubt stocked with almost every sort of chemical.

Now that really was absurd! I couldn't suspect Bill Brockton—amusing, talkative, cheerfully amorous Bill. Now I *would* stop it! Keeping my mind on the dinner I would cook—meat loaf and baked carrots and salad, with bed immediately afterward—I drove the rest of the way to the beach.

Carrying the heavy box of groceries, I started up the plank stairs, then hesitated. I set the box down, went around under the staircase, and emptied the thermos. Catching the concentrated runoff from the plank above, it must have been full to the brim an hour or so after the rain started. I picked up the thermos cap and brushed off the damp sand coating its rough surface. No hope of fingerprints, even if he hadn't worn gloves while handling the thermos, which he probably had. Placing the thermos on top of the groceries, I climbed to the sun deck.

As I unlocked the door, it occurred to me that perhaps I should have stopped at the hardware store for a bolt and chain. Perhaps I should go back and— But no. For one thing, I didn't like the thought of the covert amusement I'd see in the store owner's eyes, as he sold that New York girl a bolt to keep out the bogeyman. For another, the door already had a Yale lock, and was stout enough to resist almost any battering shoulder except that of a Baltimore Colt lineman. Besides, anyone determined upon entrance could simply smash the window and step over the sill into the living room.

No, I thought, as Howie, in anticipation of dinner, trotted ahead of me into the kitchen, I'd still rely upon my dog for my main protection. No matter that his villain-ous visage and bull-like chest were belied by a dove's heart. Even a dove, surely, fights to protect its own. I felt that, if the occasion arose, Howie would sink all six of his teeth in an intruder's leg, and hang on for as long as necessary.

I'd fed Howie, and almost finished mix-ing the meat loaf, when the phone rang. It was Gabe. "I drove over to your house about an hour and a half ago, but you weren't there."

"I was in town, grocery shopping."

For a few moments he said nothing. Even over the phone I could feel the anxious, embarrassed quality of his silence. "Look, Jane. There's a story going around that you went to see Mort Jones this morning."

"I did. And what I told him was true. I don't care how he's made it sound. It was true."

"I think I'd better go over to your place."

"No!" In the grocery store Mrs. New-combe had said, "You don't look at all well," and a few minutes ago the mirror in the bathroom had confirmed her words. I needed rest, so that I would look and behave normally when I told Gabe all about it. No matter what others thought, it was important that he be convinced that there was—nothing wrong with me. In fact, I was a bit shaken to realize just how important that was to me.

"I'm awfully tired. And I'll be all right. There's a good lock on the door, and I've got Howie." Besides, I was sure my reasoning earlier that day had been correct. Now that my abductor knew I harbored no knowledge dangerous to him, he'd no longer consider me a threat.

"Wouldn't you feel safer, here at the hotel?"

"Gabe, I'm fine. I'll see you tomorrow night."

"Well, if you're sure," he said in a reluctant voice. "Good night, Jane."

Around six-thirty, I put the meat loaf in the oven, flanking it with parboiled carrots. Almost an hour later, I ate my dinner from the glass-topped wicker table in the living room. Howie, no doubt glad that I was again taking my meals like a civilized person, lay dozing at my feet. When the dogs over in the pine grove began to yip, he gave a token growl, and then dropped his muzzle back onto his extended paws. Apparently he'd at last become convinced that the wild dogs would not venture out of their swampy fortress.

It was fully dark now. In the black windowpane, its side draperies pushed back, I could see my dim reflection. Blackness all around this house now, and no other inhabited house for at least a mile. Despite all my reasoning about the lack of any immediate danger, I found myself listening for a stealthy footfall on the plank stairs, found myself wishing I'd accepted Gabe's offer of a hotel room. Crossing to the window, I pulled the draperies closed.

That made me feel no better. It was the silence, I decided—the utter silence that was weighing upon me. Other nights, down on the sand, there'd been the soft lapping of wavelets and the friendly crackle of my driftwood fire. But, now that the dogs over in the swamp had quieted down, no sound at all came through the walls of this little house, not even the cry of some night bird, or the drone of a jet flying high above the thin overcast.

With sudden inspiration, I went into the bedroom, came back to the living room carrying my transistor radio, and tuned it to the loudest music I could find. Instantly the atmosphere seemed to change. To the accompaniment of throbbing electric guitars, sitars, and the amorous wailing of Tom Jones and the Tomcats, I carried my dishes in to the sink and rinsed them. Washing could wait until tomorrow. So tired I ached, I switched off the transistor and went to bed.

Thirteen

During the night that thin cloud cover vanished, and the temperature dropped. The next day was clear, bright, and much cooler than any I'd experienced so far on the Cape. What with a long night's sleep and a cobalt blue bay sparkling in the sunlight, I felt infinitely better.

After breakfast I completed my drawing of a sandpiper, and then began to prepare for my dinner date. I manicured my nails, and checked over the dressiest dress I'd brought with me—a brown one of light-weight wool crepe, with a scoop neck and long sleeves—to make sure it didn't need pressing. For a moment I thought of driving into Garth to see if the blond Miss Carruthers could do my hair. But no. I felt stronger, but still not strong enough to face again the townspeople's curious stares. I'd set my own hair.

After lunch, dressed in wool pants and my hooded car coat, I started north along the beach, toward a headland that appeared to be about a mile and a half away. On none of my driftwood-gathering forays had I even reached the headland, let alone gone around it. As if stimulated by the cool, sparkling air, Howie made lumbering charges at sea gulls, caught up sticks in his teeth and tossed them into the air, and, if I hadn't seized his collar in time, would have rolled in the remains of a long-dead sand shark.

We rounded the headland, with its big dunes crowned by eel grass. A few yards away, in the lee of a dune a tall heavyset man with a luxuriant black beard stood behind an easel. I guessed him to be in his late thirties. He wore paint-stained khaki pants and a red wool shirt, its sleeves rolled up despite the chill. A battered khaki hat of the sort some fishermen wear shadowed the upper half of his face. He looked so completely the popular conception of an artist—Anthony Quinn, say, as Gauguin— that I felt sure he must be a very bad painter indeed.

My unwontedly frisky dog charged him, barking. "Shut up," the man said calmly.

Wagging his stumpy tail, Howie backed off, and then made another charge, brushing against the easel's leg. "You upset this easel," the man said, in that same matter-of-fact voice, "and I'll drag you out and drown you."

Hurrying, I came up and grabbed Howie's collar. "Now you stop that!" Then, to the man: "Sorry."

He was looking down at Howie. "That's the ugliest dog I ever saw. He's so ugly he's beautiful."

With my attention riveted on his painting, I scarcely heard him. I'd been wrong about his ability. At the bottom of the canvas he'd interpreted the beach as a ragged strip of warm beige. By contrast, the bay was a cold blue, shading into a sky that was a lighter shade of blue, but still cold in tone. A ragged band of black pressed down at the top of the painting. And at the left, linking the cold blue water with that cloud-like band at the top, was a black spiral, like some demon rising from the sea.

"You're good," I said.

He'd returned his attention to his work,

thickening the base of the spiral with a brush stroke. He said, in that same calm voice in which he'd told Howie he'd drown him, "What the hell would you know about it?"

That irritated me. I said, deadpan, "I don't know much about art, but I know what I like."

He glanced at me and then, after a moment, grinned. "All right. What do you like about it?"

"I think it's the sort of painting Melville would make of the sea, if he were alive now, and a painter."

His eyes, dark and deep-set, looked at me more keenly. "Maybe you do know a little something." His face altered. "Are you that New York girl, the one who knew Laura-belle Crandall?"

"Yes."

"I heard about you when I went into town four or five days ago." He poised his brush, then dropped it with a clatter into the groove at the easel's base. "Damn it, why did you have to come along?"

It struck me, then, that he was probably Jules Laretta. Laura, lovely and still very young, and this bearded ruffian at least half a generation older. For an instant the idea seemed utterly incongruous. Then I realized that in at least one way they might have been suited. Around Laura, too, had hovered the unmistakable air of the loner.

I said coldly, "Sorry I intruded. Come along, Howie."

"No, wait. I'd made up my mind not to see you, but now that you've turned up—" He broke off, and then said, "I'm Jules Laretta."

"I guessed that."

"Did Laurabelle tell you about me?"

"Laurabelle told me almost nothing about anyone, including herself. People find that hard to believe, but it's true."

"They don't believe it because they didn't really know Laurabelle. I did." He glanced at the watch strapped to one hairy wrist. "Come on up to my house. I want you to tell me about her."

"I can tell you anything you want to know right here."

"Come *on*, damn it! I've got a stew on the stove, and it's time to put in the vegetables. You can sic your dog on me if you have to, but you won't have to."

He turned away and started up the beach, as if sure I'd follow. Half annoyed, half amused, I called, "Are you going to leave your painting here?"

He halted. "No one will bother it. Are you coming? I'll be eating that stew for the next three days, and I don't want to ruin it."

I knew nothing about him, beyond the name he'd given me, and the fact that he had bad manners, and talent. But even the bad manners were reassuring. He'd done nothing to ingratiate himself, nothing to indicate he knew he was dealing with a girl rendered frightened and suspicious by what had happened to her two nights before. Besides, he hadn't sought me out—had deliberately stayed away from me, according to him—and he'd had no way of knowing I'd decide to walk this far up the beach at this particular time.

"Who do you think I am, Jack the Ripper? All right. Go home. I'll drive over to your place later today."

"You don't have to do that. I'm coming."

He waited for me. For perhaps twenty yards we moved in silence up the beach, with Howie trotting ahead of us. Then I said, "So you know where I'm staying."

"Sure. When I was in Garth last Monday that damned blabbermouth of a doctor buttonholed me and told me a New York girl had rented Luke Carberry's place on the bay. He said that Laurabelle had been on her way to your apartment when—" He broke off. "He told me your name, but I forgot."

"It's Warren, Jane Warren."

"Here's the jeep. My place is only about a mile away."

The jeep stood, flanked by dunes, on a narrow dirt road similar to the one that led to my rented house. As I got into the high front seat, with Howie scrambling in after me, I noticed the registration slip fastened to the steering column. It was made out to Jules Laretta, all right.

He got behind the wheel, backed, and pointed the jeep's nose away from the beach. The road ahead was rough, with rain water still standing in some of the low spots. On either side marsh grass, still winter-brown, sprang from the low-lying ground. Once, disturbed by the jeep's engine, a male ring-necked pheasant flew up from the grass with a flash of iridescent greenish bronze and a machine-gun clatter of wings.

After a while I said, "Apparently you don't go in to Garth often."

"Once a week, for supplies and mail."

Then perhaps he hadn't even heard of my visit to Chief Jones. "Don't you like the people in Garth?"

He shrugged. "They're like all people. Gabble-gabble. Why do people have to tell each other it's a nice day, when any fool can see it is?"

I smiled. "Just to be friendly, I suppose."

He didn't answer. Perhaps a minute later, we turned a bend in the road. "Here's my place."

It was even plainer than my rented house. At least mine had a sun deck and a picture window. This was just a rectangular wooden box, painted gray, set on a foundation of rough cement, and topped with a peaked roof. Instead of grass, white gravel occupied the space between the house and the road. I had the feeling he'd built the house himself.

He stopped the jeep and got out. Unassisted, I too stepped down to the gravel. He'd opened the unlocked front door. "Come in."

I followed Howie over the threshold and found myself in light almost as brilliant as that outdoors. The entire rear wall of the room was of heavy plate glass, affording a view of the marshland and the beach dunes rising beyond it. To my right, just inside the door, stood a table strewn with tubes of paint, paint brushes, and paint-stained rags. Otherwise, the room was meticulously neat. In a low fireplace set in the wall to my left, two smoldering logs sent out a pleasant warmth.

He took a fresh log from the brass basket beside the hearth and added it to the fire. "Sit down. It won't take me long."

I sat down in one of a pair of those molded plastic chairs that are always so much more comfortable than they look, and Howie stretched out on the floor beside me. Through one door in the opposite wall part of a low, wide bed was visible. Through the other I could see my host standing at the sink in a small kitchen, big hands deft as he peeled a potato.

"Laurabelle was always over at Jules' place," her aunt had said. I pictured her moving about this little house, probably a far happier Laura, at least most of the time, than the one I'd known. It was strange to realize that when she went into one of her long silences in New York, she might well have been reviewing some memory of this light-flooded room with its clean pine floor, or of that bedroom, or the tiny kitchen where Jules Laretta was now uncorking a bottle of wine. He carried it out of my sight, apparently to a simmering kettle that, invisible to me, was sending out an appetizing fragrance.

He stood in the kitchen doorway. "You want a drink?"

"Thanks, but it's a little early for me."

Apparently feeling that the amenities had been satisfied, he came into the room and sat down in the chair opposite me. With a slight shock, I saw that his deep-set eyes looked wretched.

"All right. Tell me about Laurabelle, from the time you met her, on."

I told him, omitting only that she'd said, when she gave me the bracelet, "I've decided that there's no *point* in my keeping it." Somehow I couldn't tell him that. As I was speaking of how I'd gone alone to that cemetery in Queens, he got up abruptly, walked over to the glass wall, and stood staring out, back turned.

At last he said, not turning, "And she seemed very unhappy?"

Surely he knew she'd been, from all I'd said in the past ten minutes. "More than that. She seemed—haunted." I paused. "Had—had there been trouble between you two before she left here?"

"No more than usual." He fell silent for a moment, and then said, "Oh, hell. You've got a right to know, if anyone has. I have a wife down in Florida. Laurabelle kept nagging me to get a divorce, so she and I could get married."

"Mightn't it have been a good idea?" I was aware of the coldness in my voice.

"No. I haven't anything against my wife. I just haven't lived with her for the last ten years, that's all. Besides, a divorce would have been tough to manage. She'd never have divorced me—she's a devout Catholic—and if I'd divorced her she'd never have forgiven me. She's told me so."

After a moment he added, "I've got two boys. I'm welcome to visit them at any time. I wanted to keep it that way."

I said, with rising anger, "But was that fair to Laurabelle?"

He swung around. "Fair to Laurabelle? Why, we were in love! She was damned happy. We both were, except whenever she started talking about a divorce."

"Don't you realize that love isn't enough

for most women? They want marriage, children—"

He said violently, "What do you know about what Laurabelle and I had? What do you know about love, you silly little virgin?"

After a moment I said, "I am neither silly nor little. As for my being a virgin, you don't know whether I am or not, do you?"

He opened his mouth to say something, and then apparently decided against it. At last he said, "Peppery sort, aren't you?"

"Sometimes."

"All right. I'm sorry." From the obvious effort those last two words cost him, I guessed he seldom apologized to anyone for anything. He came over and sat down again. "Who gave you the idea there'd been a row between Laurabelle and me just before she ran away?"

"Laurabelle's aunt."

"That bitch."

"She told me that Laurabelle came home looking very upset. She'd been with you, or at least Mrs. Newcombe assumed she had been. The next day Laurabelle left, while her aunt was taking a nap."

"Laurabelle was upset all right, the last time I saw her, but it wasn't because of a quarrel." Pain crossed his face. "I don't know what it was. I've gone over it all a hundred times in my mind, and I still can't figure it out."

He explained, then, that Laurabelle had driven to his house that afternoon in an old jalopy that he himself had given her. "I had to go up to Provincetown for some canvas and oils, and I asked her if she wanted to go with me. She said no, she'd stay here and make a chowder for our dinner out of the clams I'd dug the day before. When I came back she was burning something here in the fireplace.

"Burning something?"

"A few minutes later she told me it had been a paper towel she had used to mop up spilled bacon grease in the kitchen. Maybe it had been. I didn't get close enough to the fireplace to see, because the minute I came in the door she moved across the room to me and said she had a terrible headache and wanted to go home. She certainly looked sick, white as a sheet."

"Did she go home?"

"Yes. I was worried, and wanted to drive her home myself, but she wouldn't let me. Later that evening I phoned her, even though she didn't like for me to do that.

Her aunt gave her a bad time whenever I did. Laurabelle herself answered the phone, and said she felt much better. She didn't sound sick then. Just—remote. She'd phone me the next day, she said."

"But she didn't?"

"No. And the day after that, when I drove to the post office in Garth, there was a letter from her. It said she was leaving town and never coming back, and that even if I managed to find her, she'd have nothing more to do with me. I called her aunt immediately, and she said yes, Laurabelle had run away. How she must have enjoyed telling me that!"

"Well, you could scarcely expect her to approve of you."

"Of course not." He gave a short, sardonic laugh. "I suppose I'd have been damned shocked if she hadn't disapproved of me. No, that's not why I called her a bitch. It's because she's cold and mean, clear through. I never knew Ed Newcombe, the man who married and brought her here. He died long before I came to the Cape. I've always wondered, though, how he could have done it. But then, some men are attracted to that type of woman."

Fleetingly I thought of Luke Carberry.

"Then there was no big final quarrel between you and Laurabelle?"

"Nothing even resembling it. Look. She'd made the clam chowder. I found it cooking on the stove. Does a girl spend half the afternoon fixing a man's favorite dish, and then suddenly decide she never wants to see him again?"

"I wouldn't think so."

He hunched his shoulders miserably. "A few days after she left, it hit me that maybe she'd found some old letter lying around, and something in it had upset her."

"Letter?"

"A love letter, from some girl I'd known before I met her. Not that I kept such stuff. I'd always figured that when something was over it was over, and there was no point in giving house room to mementos. Still, I thought there might have been one I'd neglected to throw out."

"Perhaps there was. Perhaps that's what she was burning."

"I thought of that. But it wouldn't have been like her not to say anything about it. If something in it had hurt her, or angered her, or even disgusted her, she'd have told me about it, straight out. She was reserved with others, but not with me. Until that last

169

day, I think she and I were about as frank as two human beings can be with each other.

"No," he went on, "I don't think she found a letter or anything. And that leaves me stuck with the conclusion that she really did suddenly decide she couldn't take the situation any longer. She must have felt it so strongly she didn't even want to discuss it with me. Instead she just—left." One hand tightened over the knee of his paint-stained trousers. "If I'd known she was going to do that, I'd have given in to her about the divorce."

For perhaps a minute there was no sound except the crackle of the fire. Then I asked, "Have you any idea why she should have felt frightened that night, just before she was killed?"

He shook his head. "Not," he said wryly, "unless she saw someone she thought was me. That might have upset her, if she'd left here simply because she wanted to cut me out of her life. But it couldn't have been me. I'd given up, by that time."

"Given up?"

"Looking for her. I felt she'd head for a big city. Most people do when they want to disappear. I hired a Boston detective, for as long as I could afford him. He couldn't trace her past Sagamore, where she transferred to a Boston bus. I myself went to Boston twice, and down to New York for three days once. I knew I was being a fool, but I figured there might be one chance in a million."

I thought of him in New York, this strange, selfish man, who hadn't discovered how much he loved until his girl had left him. He must have ridden the subways, wandered through the Village and Washington Square, moved through the lunchtime crowds in midtown and Wall Street, his deepset eyes looking and looking for that one face in eight million.

I said, "I still have her bracelet. Do you want it back?"

"Keep it." His voice was rough. "She's dead, isn't she? What do I want with her bracelet?"

"All right. I'll keep it."

"And you'd do me a favor by taking some other stuff she left here. I've wanted to throw it out, but somehow—"

Without waiting for my reply, he went into the bedroom and came back with her "stuff," almost a dozen hardcover and paperbacked books. He said, handing them to me, "Elizabeth Barrett Browning and Rupert Brooke! I used to tell her she was a throwback, and why wasn't she reading Ginsberg?"

Yes, I thought. An admirer of *Howl* might have been more tolerant of the situation than a girl who liked to read, "How do I love thee? Let me count the ways." But I didn't say it. After all, in *his* way, he'd loved her.

I looked at the books. Hardcover copies of Brooke, Millay, and Elizabeth Barrett Browning. A paperbacked copy of *The Oxford Book of English Verse*. The other paperbacks, surprisingly, had titles like *Dead Men Tell No Lies*, and *Case of the Vanishing Detective.*

He must have seen my surprise. "Didn't you know she was hooked on that stuff, too?"

"No." Laura had never mentioned to me that she liked detective stories. But then, there was a lot she hadn't mentioned.

"In Boston," he said, "there's a shop that sells used paperbacks two for a quarter, and buys them back for five cents apiece. Every time Laura went to Boston for shopping, she took a load of paperbacks with her, and brought another load back. Anyway, you take them, huh?"

He hadn't been able to throw out any of these books, not even *They Murdered for Profit*, because Laurabelle's hands had touched them. "I'm pleased to have her books. And I think I'd better go home now."

He didn't demur. Probably he wanted to get rid of me, now that we'd talked, just as he wanted to rid himself of the other reminders of Laura. "I'll drive you home. It would be a long walk."

"Thank you."

We went out to the jeep. Through mid-afternoon sunlight, we continued along the road that ran past his house, and then turned right onto a road that led past stands of pitch pine and an occasional house. Most of the houses looked fairly new, although of traditional Cape Cod design, but now and then we passed an eighteenth-century house, or a bay-windowed Victorian house, like Mrs. Newcombe's dark red one.

I said, "Then Mrs. Newcombe's husband lived on the Cape before he married her?"

"He was born here. It's an old family. There are Newcombes all over the Cape."

"But he didn't marry her here?"

"No. He'd been told by a Boston heart

specialist that he probably had only a few more years to live. He was in his early thirties then. Maybe he wanted to make the most of the time he had left. Anyway, he started traveling. He could afford it. His branch of the Newcombes had money."

"Where did he meet Laurabelle's aunt?"

"In France, somewhere. She and her sister—Laurabelle's mother, I mean—had taken Laurabelle and gone from Canada to France, for some reason or another. He met that woman, and married her, and brought her and her sister and Laurabelle back to the Cape. Laurabelle didn't remember coming here, of course. She wasn't much more than a baby."

"When did her mother die?"

"When Laurabelle was three. Cancer. She must have been sick with it even before she came to Garth. And about a year later Ed Newcombe died."

He gave a short laugh. "He must have found out what his wife was like before he died, because he didn't leave her all his money with no strings attached. He provided a trust fund with part of his estate. It paid Mrs. Newcombe three hundred a month—but only so long as Laurabelle lived with her. After that, the fund would go to the Cape Cod Historical Society. If he hadn't done that, she'd have managed to get Laurabelle out of the house years ago."

I'd wondered about that, from time to time, ever since my interview with Mrs. Newcombe. Certainly she'd displayed no love for her niece. And yet she'd allowed her to remain in the Newcombe house, even after Laurabelle's conduct had provided her with an excuse to turn the girl out. Now I knew why.

Well, at least she hadn't profited by Laura's flight, nor by her death. Instead, she'd lost three hundred a month, which was a nice bit of extra income, even these days.

Laura's death. As the jeep turned onto the narrow road that led directly to my place, I was aware of a growing sense of guilt. Because I'd been Laura's friend during the last lonely months of her life, Jules Laretta had talked of her with a frankness that must have been both unusual and painful for him. I hadn't been equally frank. I hadn't told him that I had reason to think that Laura had been killed—deliberately murdered—by someone here on the Cape.

I felt I couldn't talk about that. My

nightmarish experience, and Chief Jones's derision of my account of it, were still painfully fresh in my mind. Speaking of it now would upset me badly. And I mustn't be upset. When I talked to Gabe tonight, I must appear calm, completely rational. It would be terrible to see in Gabe's eyes the disbelief I'd seen in Chief Jones's.

And yet surely I owed Jules Laretta whatever comfort I could give him. When he stopped the jeep at the end of the road, between the grass-crowned dunes, I turned to him and said, "I don't think she ran away because she was—fed up. I think there was some other reason. In fact, I feel sure of it."

The deep-set eyes regarded me for a moment. "I'm glad you were Laurabelle's friend," he said, and reached across me to unfasten the jeep's door.

Fourteen

By the time Gabe arrived, I'd set my hair and brushed it until it shone. I'd tried both a chain necklace and an antique jet one, which had belonged to a great-aunt of mine, with the scooped neck dress, and then decided I looked better with no jewelry at all. I'd put on coral lipstick, rubbed it off, and rouged my mouth a very pale pink. I'd applied eye shadow, which I seldom do, and daubed my best perfume behind my ears and in the hollow of my throat.

When I opened the door to Gabe's knock, I knew it had been worth all that work. His gaze said, "You look wonderful," even before he put it into words.

Obviously he'd taken pains with his appearance, too. Instead of the khaki shirt and pants that seemed almost a masculine uniform up here, he wore a dark suit which looked as if it had come from Madison Avenue. Probably it had. His tie was a conservative gray and red stripe, and the sun-streaked hair topping his homely handsome face had been freshly trimmed.

He said, "All set?" and held my coat for me.

In the Ford station wagon, we drove through lingering twilight to the highway running through Garth. As we turned right, he asked abruptly, "Do you want to tell me about the other night now, or after dinner?"

"Afterwards, if you don't mind."

If possible, I'd prove during dinner that I was more than just reasonably pleasant to the eye. I'd show what a fascinating companion I could be, intelligent without being stuffy, and witty without being malicious.

The Dennisport restaurant we went to occupied the lower floor of an old mansion, set on a tree-lined street of similar houses. The dining room, paneled in walnut, was hung with oil landscapes. The round tables, set pleasantly far apart, bore vases of daffodils and fat candles set in bowls of ruby glass. A man pianist—there only on weekends, Gabe told me —played unobtrusively the sort of music always played in such places, *Stardust,* and *Artist's Life,* and *The Third Man Theme.*

The setting was perfect. And yet from the start, that dinner was a quiet little disaster.

Oh, I tried. I asked him what branch of engineering he'd studied at Columbia. (Always show an intelligent interest in a man's work.) When he replied that his degree was in mechanical engineering, I told him about a cartoon I'd seen in which a couple of engineers watched a bridge collapse. "You were right about that blueprint," one of the engineers was saying. "That was a flyspeck instead of a decimal point."

I spoke briefly and I hoped entertainingly about a recent Czech movie I'd seen. ("Do you get foreign films up here in the summer? You must look forward to them.") I asked questions about the Cape's geology and history, and listened raptly to his answers.

He too tried. He laughed at my little joke about the bridge, and answered all my questions. But it was no go. Our smiles were forced, our voices strained. The subject we hadn't discussed seemed to hover above the table like a small black cloud.

At last, while we were having coffee, he asked, "Want to talk about it now?"

I gave a light little laugh. "The funny part of it is that what frightened me most was the next morning. I thought I'd gone insane."

Then, to my horror, my throat closed up, and hot tears pressed behind my eyes. Biting my lower lip, I sent him a look of mute appeal. "We'll get out of here," he said, and signaled the waitress.

I managed to keep those tears back while we walked out to the parking lot. But the instant I was inside the station wagon, I began to sob uncontrollably, my hands covering my face. He gave my shoulder a comforting squeeze, and then started the engine.

A few minutes later he stopped the car opposite a vacant lot on a dark, tree-lined street, and drew me to him. "All right. Let it all out."

Against his shoulder, I cried for several minutes more, while he stroked my hair and made soothing noises. At last I sat up, blew my nose on the large handkerchief he handed me, and gave a little laugh.

"What is it?"

"Oh, just a silly idea that struck me. God was pretty rough on Eve. But at least he made a man's shoulder wide enough to cry on."

"Be my guest, anytime." He paused. "Ready to tell me now?"

I told him, in a voice hoarse from crying. At last I said, "I wouldn't blame you for thinking I imagined the whole thing."

"I don't think that."

He spoke so forcibly that I knew, feeling wretched, that he did have his doubts. Then he said, "The thing to do is to find that house."

Of course! Finding the house would not only convince him of the reality of my experience. It would banish the frightened little doubt that sometimes quivered through my own mind.

"You have no idea in what direction you were taken, or how far?"

"No."

"Well, it was almost certainly somewhere on the Cape. Otherwise it's highly unlikely that he'd have been able to take you there, question you, and bring you back before daylight. Was it an empty house?"

"I think so. All the furniture I can remember is the chair I sat in, and this old table with the candle on it. And on the other side of the room there must have been another chair, the one the—the—"

"Yes," he said quickly. "Was there a fireplace?"

I concentrated. It seemed to me that I'd been aware of a yawning space in the wall at my left. "I think so."

"Was it an old house?"

"I don't know for sure. I had the feeling it was."

"What was the floor like?"

"I don't remember looking at the floor."

"The windows?"

"Little panes. I remember the reflection of the candle in all those squares of glass."

"Well, that doesn't help much. Any house up here built before the middle of the last century is apt to have those little windowpanes. What's more, builders put such panes in new houses to make them look quaint."

"The house wasn't new."

"How can you be sure?"

After a moment I said, "It didn't smell new." It seemed to me now that the air in the room had been redolent of ancient timbers, and of many hundreds of fires which had blazed and died in that yawning space at my left, and of mildew.

He nodded. "Old houses do have a different smell, especially if they haven't aired for quite some time. Did he break in?"

I remembered the grate of metal against metal, painful to my sharpened hearing, and what sounded like the rattle of a chain, and then the creak of hinges. "He must have had a key, maybe two of them. I mean, I think there was a padlock on the door."

"Let's go back a little. That laugh you heard from somewhere outside the car. Could it have been a loon? We get them up here."

"I don't know. I've never heard a loon."

"They sound like madmen on the loose. If you heard one, you were somewhere near the shore. The Nauset Marsh, perhaps. And that hollow sound you mentioned hearing, just before you got to the house, might fit in with marshy land. You could have been passing over a bridge."

"A bridge?"

"Over some streamlet winding through the marsh." Then, worriedly: "The trouble is there aren't many roads through the marshy areas, or houses either. Not enough solid ground to build on. But we'll start looking. We'll start tomorrow, and keep on until we find it."

"But your hotel, the repairs—"

"The Dudleys can take care of any guests who show up. And the repairs are well enough along that I don't have to supervise."

Were they, or was he just being generous? "Oh, Gabe! I don't know how to—"

"Then don't try." He paused. "Don't you think you'd better move over to the hotel?"

"I don't think there's any danger, not now. And I've got Howie."

I had still another reason for wanting to stay in my rented house. I was on the rebound. If I stayed at the hotel, things might move too fast between Gabe and me. I didn't want that. Oh, I liked what I knew of him, but I didn't know him well yet. And I had no intention of finding myself deeply involved with another Kevin Doyle.

His voice was reluctant. "Well, it's up to you. But still—" He broke off, and then said, "Do you feel up to a drink now, and perhaps a little dancing? There's a place between here and Garth that has a good combo on weekends."

"Well, I—Just a minute."

I took out my compact and, by the dashboard's light, made an appalled inspection of my face, with its smeared mascara and tear-reddened nose. "Thank you, but I'd better stay in the dark. I look like the last act of *Pagliacci*."

"You're a mess," he agreed, "but on you it doesn't look bad." Reaching over, he opened the glove compartment, took out some paper tissues, and handed them to me. "Anyway, it's good to find out."

"What?" I dabbed at the mascara smeared under my eyes.

"How a girl looks when she's been crying, or has a head cold."

Somehow that sounded more warmly promising than half a dozen romantic speeches.

Except for Steve and Grace's Tavern, and a few houses whose windows showed the blue glow of TV sets, Garth seemed already asleep when we entered it. We drove the length of Main Street. Then, to my surprise, Gabe stopped in front of the hotel.

"I won't be long."

A few minutes later he emerged from the hotel, carrying something in his right hand. As he got into the car, I saw, shying away,

185

that it was a gun. Reaching across me, he placed it in the glove compartment.

"That's for you. You're to keep it right beside your bed."

"Oh, no! I've never even touched a gun. I'd be more afraid of it than of—"

"It's not dangerous, as long as the safety's on. I'll show you how to use it."

About fifteen minutes later, in the living room of my rented house, he did show me. "This is an automatic, thirty-two caliber, and it's fully loaded. Unless you intend to use it, don't move the safety catch—that's this little gadget here—and always keep it pointed at the floor, the way I am now."

He showed me how to snap the safety catch on and off, and to load and unload the cartridge clip that held the bullets. "Now you try it."

Gingerly, I did. "That's fine." He took the gun from me. "Is there a table beside your bed?"

"A nightstand, with a drawer."

He went into the bedroom. I heard the shallow little drawer open and close. "Okay," he said, returning to me, "it's there if you need it."

He laughed. "You didn't get all of the mascara. You look as if you've got two shiners." Hands on my shoulders, he kissed me lightly. I liked that. He kissed me again, not so lightly, and I liked that even better.

"Will nine tomorrow be too early for you?"

"No."

"I'll pick you up then."

Fifteen

The next day—another cool bright one, with fleecy clouds drifting across a deep blue sky—had the look and feel and sound of Sunday. In Garth, men and boys in dark suits, and women with well-brushed coats over print dresses, moved along the sidewalks. Little girls, after the fashion of little girls when wearing their best, looked inordinately pleased with themselves, and their flowered straw hats, and their small shoulder bags of white plastic. Somewhere up the street on which Mrs. Newcombe lived, a church bell tolled. And except for the pharmacy, every business establishment on Main Street was closed.

By two in the afternoon, we'd searched the marshy area bordering Nauset Bay, on the Atlantic side of the Cape, with no success whatsoever. Most of the few houses in that region of brown meadow grass and meandering streamlets were obviously occupied, with curtains at the windows and smoke rising from chimneys. Of the unoccupied houses, some were set on stilts, like my own rented house. Others were too close to the road. To reach their doors, we wouldn't have had to cross a stretch of tall vegetation, such as I could remember whipping at my legs that night.

Finally Gabe stopped at the roadside. "No use looking here any more. Shall we go up toward Provincetown?"

"I don't know," I said, trying not to sound too depressed. He'd smiled as he spoke, but I'd seen the worried doubt in his eyes.

"Listen!"

From somewhere nearby came a chilling sound, laughter that suggested a manic-depressive in the elated state. "Is that what you heard that night?"

"I don't think so. It wasn't as—as human-sounding as that. And it was just two notes, one up, one down, repeated several times."

"Well, if it wasn't a loon, the house isn't

necessarily near the water. It could be anywhere." He started the engine. "Let's go north."

A little before six, we turned back toward Garth. Neither of us said much, as we moved along past pitch pines whose dark green needles looked faintly bronze in the sunset light. In the past hours we'd driven over what seemed to me dozens of intersecting roads, through stands of pine and oak, and past houses, some in groups, some isolated, some at least two hundred years old, some so new that their windows still bore X's of sticking tape.

Once, for a few heart-racing minutes, I'd thought we'd found the house. It had sat back from the road, behind a gateless and broken picket fence. Its lawn was a mass of dried weeds. A tall, rectangular house of the sort built in the first half of the nineteenth century, it had once been yellow. Now its clapboards were scabrous with peeling paint. True, we'd crossed no bridge just before we reached it. But my time sense undoubtedly had been distorted that night. Perhaps in reality there'd been a considerable interval between the time I heard that kettledrum noise beneath the car's wheels and the time I was propelled, stumbling, through rain-drenched weeds. And this house certainly did have small-paned windows, and a long porch that was only one step up. Aware of my quickened pulses, I moved beside Gabe up a walk of broken flagstones.

The door, parts of its fanlight glass missing, was padlocked. At windows, cracked green shades hid the rooms beyond. Gabe said, "Let's go around to the side."

On the south side of the house, two little panes in the lower half of a window had been broken, with shards of glass still protruding from the frames. After bringing gloves from the car, Gabe picked out some of the shards, reached his arm carefully inside the opening, and groped for the pull ring at the bottom of the shade. Finding it, he let the shade roll up about a foot, and then withdrew his arm.

Bleakly I stared into the room. Bathed in greenish light, an old brown sofa, its springs sagging to a threadbare flowered carpet, stood flanked by a cheap scarred end table and a tall standing lamp, its fringed shade of faded green silk askew.

"No, this isn't the house. There was no furniture like that, and no carpet." I could remember the sound of footsteps over a

191

bare floor, as the raincoated figure moved past me toward the other side of the room.

"Besides," Gabe said, peering in, "the fireplace is in the wrong place. If you'd sat here the way you described to me, with the front door on your right, you'd have been facing the fireplace."

Reaching in, he'd pulled the cracked blind down. We'd returned in silence to the car.

Now, as we approached Garth, Gabe said, "Don't look so discouraged. There's still a lot of territory to cover. I'd better stick close to the hotel in the mornings next week, but we can search in the afternoons."

I blurted, "Be honest. You don't think it happened, do you?"

After a moment he said, "I'm sure you think it happened. Maybe it did. We'll know for certain if we find that house."

"And if we don't, what will be your advice? See my friendly neighborhood psychiatrist?" I'd tried to make the words sound light, but my voice shook.

His hand left the wheel briefly to squeeze my hand. "Now what's the point of talking about that at this stage of the game? Would you like to have dinner at the hotel tonight? It'll be roast beef."

"I'd like to very much." I'd been dreading the thought of dinner off that glass-topped table, with no company except Howie, and my reflection in the black windowpane, and my depressed thoughts.

"I'll have to feed Howie, though." Because it was sometimes hard to get him back into a car after a brief stop, I'd decided to leave him at home.

"All right. We'll go to your place first."

Sixteen

During the next four afternoons we combed roads—asphalt ones, dirt ones, and some that were little more than tracks through the woods—around Truro, and Wellfleet and, eventually, south toward Eastham. The old house with the many-paned windows remained elusive—as elusive, I began to feel, as if it had no existence outside my memory of it.

Our excursions didn't go unobserved, of course. Twice Senator Carberry, with a broad smile and a wave of his hand, passed us in his big gray car. On its bumper was a sticker bearing his slogan for the primary campaign: *The Cranberry and Carberry—the Cape Needs Them Both.* Several times we encountered Mr. Dudley, out on errands in the hotel's pickup truck, and twice he and Gabe stopped to confer for a few minutes. Once Mrs. Newcombe, with Dr. Rainey beside her at the wheel, passed us in her well-kept Lincoln. She turned her cold, amused smile in our direction, and nodded. We met Miss Carruthers and Mary Manwell, too, driving along in a battered sedan which, Gabe told me, belonged to the hairdresser. Miss Manwell, apparently, had decided to forgive my friendship with the girl she'd so bitterly disliked, because her melancholy face broke into a faint smile when she saw us, and both she and her companion waved.

I realized that Gabe and I must have become a nightly topic of gossip at Steve and Grace's Tavern. But that seemed a small consideration, compared to our failure to find that house. It became harder and harder for me to conceal my apprehensive gloom, but I tried. If Gabe was going to remember me as that nutty New York girl who'd come up here one April, I told myself grimly, at least he was going to remember me as a fairly cheerful nut.

We had dinner together, one night at my place, and the other nights at the hotel. By tacit consent, we didn't discuss our search during those meals, but instead talked of our separate pasts, and of his plans for his future as an engineer, and of my book of sketches and little rhymes, which I'd scarcely worked on for a week now.

One night in the hotel dining room I told him of my conversation with Jules Laretta. Gabe said, "I gather you like him."

"I did, rather. Oh, I think he's a colossally selfish man, but I think he's an honest one, too. I believed him when he said that there'd been no big final quarrel between him and Laurabelle."

I'd spoken a shade apprehensively, but I saw no leap of remembered pain in Gabe's eyes. After a moment he said, "If there was a quarrel, maybe it was between her and her aunt. I guess we'll never know.

"Poor little Laurabelle," he added, after a moment. "I can remember her when she was seven, walking around with a chipmunk on her shoulder. She'd rescued it from a cat, and tamed it. Two other eleven-year-old boys and I teased her about it, rotten little finks that we were." He paused. "She was beautiful, even then."

"Was her mother beautiful?"

"Yes, even though she must have been already dying when I first saw her. I remember her as looking almost exactly as Laurabelle did after she grew up."

"Who was Laurabelle's father?"

"I think I'd heard once that he'd been an insurance salesman. Anyway, he was killed in a car crash before Laurabelle was born."

And when she was three, her mother had died, leaving her in the care of a cold-eyed woman who almost surely had never felt affection for her. No wonder that, growing up unloved, she'd set small value on herself, so small that she'd carried on an affair with a man who gave her no hope that he'd ever marry her.

The next night, after our sixth day of fruitless search, Gabe suggested at dinner that we drive down to the tavern near Eastham, the one that provided dancing on weekends. I accepted and, to my surprise, thoroughly enjoyed dancing to the music of a combo made up of Boston University students. It was around midnight when Gabe left me at my house and drove away.

I was hanging my coat in the closet when the phone rang. A remembered voice said, "How are you doing up there in the land of the bean and the cod?"

"Bill! Are you still down in New Jersey?"

"Yes, and I've been calling you since

197

eight o'clock."

"I was in Eastham."

"With Gabe Harmon?"

"How did you know?"

"Big Brother is watching you. His eyes are everywhere."

"Come off it. How did you know?"

"I've had to phone Woods Hole several times. One of the fellows there knows Gabe. He passed along word that Gabe has been seen driving around for several days running. He had a girl of your description with him, and sometimes the world's home-liest mutt."

"That's sheer slander. I'm sure that there are at least a dozen dogs in the world homelier than mine."

"What have you two been looking for? Not a house building site, I hope."

I said, after a moment, "Just sightsee-ing." If I decided to tell Bill Brockton all about it, it wouldn't be over the long distance phone.

"Well, usually I'm not one to knock my competition, but I think you should know. The man's a paid Communist agitator."

I laughed. "I'll keep that in mind."

"Seriously, Jane, Harmon's all right, but I'm better. Older, for one thing. I read somewhere that at thirty-two a man's at his best. Still young, and yet mature, responsible, dependable. Now you think about that. Keep thinking about it until I see you, about a week from now."

"I'll do that."

We batted nonsense back and forth for a few minutes more, and then hung up. Feeling almost lighthearted, I went into the bedroom and undressed. After a week of frustrating search, this pleasant evening— first the hours at the place in Eastham, and then Bill's bantering phone call—seemed like a good omen.

Only a few hours later, the crashing invasion of my living room by some object jerked me up through layers of sleep.

For a moment I just lay there, hearing Howie's wild barks, and, in my mind's ear, the remembered crash and tinkle of glass. Then I reached out to the lamp on the bedside stand, and turned the switch.

Light flooded the bedroom and spilled through the open door into the living room. I saw it lying on the floor, an object about the size of a baseball, but irregular in shape. It was wrapped in brown paper. Beyond it, toward the living room's northern wall, glass fragments glittered.

For a moment the sight of that object which had invaded my little house brought me more outrage than fear. Then I realized that there'd been someone out there in the night. Perhaps he was still there, staring up at my lighted window—

With the little drum of fear starting up inside me, I switched off the light, got out of bed, and groped for my robe, lying over a chair back. I crossed to the bedroom window facing the bay. The half moon that had shone in the western sky as Gabe and I drove back from Eastham apparently had set, because only starlight glimmered on the pale beach. It was enough to show me, though, that no dark figure stood there, face upturned. Perhaps the object had been thrown from the north side of the house.

Jerking the draperies closed at the bedroom window, I started toward the living room, and then remembered that broken glass. I groped under the bed, found my slippers, and thrust my feet into them.

Unlike the pitch-dark bedroom, the living room, with its undrawn draperies, was filled with faint light. Yes, it was through the smaller window, the one on the north, that the object had been hurled. I could feel chill air eddying through the break. I crossed to the shattered window and looked down. No one visible out there on the sand that sloped down toward the water, nor beside my little car, up there between the dunes. But plainly, since no other car was visible, the man who'd broken the window was somewhere nearby, perhaps lurking up there behind my car, or even almost directly below me, under the sun deck—

Heart thudding, I drew the draperies, both at the broken window and the large one overlooking the bay. I switched on the overhead light. Its glare made me no safer, but it made me feel safer. Apparently it had the same effect on Howie, because his wild barks gave way to a rumbling growl.

Inwardly shrinking, I picked up the object. It was wrapped in ordinary butcher's paper, secured by two rubber bands. Stripping off the paper, I found what I'd expected to, a rock. It was of some dark red material—sandstone, probably—and speckled with white. I'd seen similar rocks on several Cape Cod beaches.

The wrapping paper had fallen to the floor. I picked it up. Two words, printed in lead pencil, seemed to leap up at me. "Go home."

I stared at the crudely printed message. It

was so childish, somehow. It was hard to believe that the person who'd hurled that rock was the same one who, in that elusive old house, had extracted from my drugged and acquiescent mind the information he needed. And yet surely the two events were connected.

Childish.

I thought of the children's game, Hide the Thimble. The child who is "It" searching under sofa cushions, behind draperies, inside vases. And the other children chanting, "You're cold, cold," or "You're getting warm!"

Hope mingled with my alarm and outrage. Was that the second—and inadvertent—meaning of this hurtled message? That Gabe and I were getting warm? No rocks had crashed through my windows as long as we confined our search to the paved roads, dirt roads, and woodcutter's tracks north of Garth. But now that we'd turned our attention southward—

Moving swiftly into the bedroom, I turned on the lamp and looked at my traveling clock. Almost five. Would anyone be on duty at the police station in Garth? Surely, even in a village of this size, there'd be someone to answer the phone in Chief

Jones's office at any hour.

I went into the living room. Just as I reached for the phone on its stand beside the bookcase, I heard a sound, fairly distant and yet distinct in the pre-dawn stillness. A car, starting up somewhere on the narrow dirt road that led to this house. Rapidly, the sound dwindled away.

The chances were excellent that the car was being driven by the rock thrower. If someone could start from Jones's office immediately, he might pass the other car on his way here, and recognize its driver.

I dialed the operator, asked for the Garth police, and a moment later heard a young but official-sounding voice. "Chief Jones's office. Jim Bledsoe speaking."

"This is Jane Warren. I'm living in Senator Carberry's house down on the bay. A rock's just been thrown through my window. Will you please send someone here right away?"

"I'm sorry, miss, but there's no one to send. I'm alone here, and I can't leave until Carl Mason comes on duty at six. But say. I could call Chief Jones."

"But it's not even five o'clock!"

"He'll be up. He's got this new retriever he's training for duck hunting. Been getting up before daylight for more than a month now."

"All right. Thank you."

I hung up. Wryly I reflected that even if Jim Bledsoe's information about the retriever were correct, Chief Jones wouldn't be happy about the interruption. And if he'd chosen to stay in bed this morning, his response to his assistant's call would be black indeed.

But when he arrived half an hour later, just as the sky was growing light, he seemed calm, courteous, and even affable. He inspected the rock and the wrapping paper, measured the distance between the floor and the jagged hole in the windowpane, and asked me to indicate where the rock had landed.

"Well, Miss Warren, with a rock it's harder to estimate a trajectory than it is with a bullet." No "Janie" this morning. "But I'd say he stood about thirty feet north of the house. I'll go down there and look for footprints, but I'm not apt to find anything plain enough to help, not in dry sand."

What had changed his manner toward me? Surely it must have been my association with Gabe. A lone girl from New York, staying on the Cape for a brief time, was one thing. But that same girl, befriended by a member of an old Cape family and the owner of the town's only hotel, was quite another.

He asked, "Any idea who did this?"

"No. No more than I know who dragged me off the beach that night."

His eyes flickered. "Now, Miss Warren, you got to admit I had a right to be skeptical about that, especially when you couldn't give me anything to go on. But I've kept my eyes and ears open since then. Haven't learned anything, though."

He paused. When I didn't comment, he went on, "But about this rock. I got a hunch some kid threw it. He got the idea, probably, from that other thing you said— that other business that scared you. I mean, word of it probably got around, somehow."

Somehow!

"You know how kids are," he went on. "They get the idea some person living alone is scared, and they try to make that person even more scared."

There seemed to be no point in arguing about it. "Did you meet any cars on your way here?"

"Come to think of it, the only car I saw

was a gas company truck. It was coming through Garth, headed for Provincetown. Why?"

I told him about hearing a car start up.

"Well, it could have turned the other way when it got to the intersection at the head of this road—that is, if it had ever been on this road. Anyway, that car probably had nothing to do with it. I'll bet any amount some kid threw that rock. Left his bike up on the road somewhere, sneaked down here to throw the rock, and then scooted."

He paused, and then added, "But maybe that's good advice printed on this paper. I mean, seems to me you'd be scared, a girl living here all alone."

There'd been a touch of the old malice in his voice. I said, "I'm not in the least scared." That was true, now that daylight had come. I was still mad, but not scared. That rock had been thrown only to frighten me, not harm me. And that meant, I was sure, that the rock thrower himself was scared, so scared that he'd made a silly, futile gesture.

"I arranged to occupy this place for four weeks," I went on, "and I intend to do just that."

"Well, you'd better be ready to move out

on the dot. Luke Carberry's promised this place to Oscar Yerxa and his wife for the summer, rent free."

I said, impressed, "He must think a lot of them."

"Does he! Oscar Yerxa's the state party leader, that's all." Again his malice flashed, although this time not at me. "Old Luke's in a real sweat. Reminds me of a bride whose mother-in-law is coming to dinner for the first time. Well, I'll go down and see if I can find any footprints."

A few minutes later he climbed the stairs. There were no footprints clear enough to be of any use, he said. Taking the rock and the wrapping paper with him, he went away.

I let Howie out for his morning ramble, cooked my breakfast, and ate. By then, sunlight was flooding the little house. Glancing at my watch, I saw that it was six-thirty. Gabe would be up.

I phoned the hotel. Gabe himself answered on the fourth ring, and I told him what had happened.

"I'll be right over," he said. Then: "No, wait. Have you got a yardstick?"

"A measuring tape, in my sewing kit."

"Measure the inside of the window frame. I'll pick up a pane of the right size at the hardware store, and put the glass in. You might have to wait days before anyone else would get around to doing it for you."

When I'd made the measurements and given them to him over the phone, I asked, "Do you think Chief Jones is right about it having been some kid?"

"I don't know. But if it wasn't, then maybe we've started to search the right area. I mean," he said, and I could hear the tension in his voice, "I think we may be getting warm, Janie."

Seventeen

We might have found the house that very same day, if Gabe hadn't decided upon strong security measures. But when he arrived around eight o'clock, he unloaded more than window glass from the station wagon. He'd also brought several wide pine boards, a power saw, a tool chest, and a cardboard box which turned out to hold hinges and thumb latches. All of these items he placed on the sun deck just outside the shattered window. I was going to have shutters, he informed me, at the windows on three sides of the house. And I was to close and lock them, from the inside, as soon as it got dark.

I cried, "But I won't have any air!"

"You can leave the kitchen window

open. There's no sun deck there."

"Gabe, you can't put shutters on another man's house."

"I've called Luke about it, and he's delighted. He'd been planning to put shutters on. I'm saving him the expense."

Fretting and fuming over the delay, I handed him nails, hammers, screwdrivers, and the putty knife for several hours. It wasn't until he'd finished the job, around one-thirty in the afternoon, that we headed down the Cape. And after two fruitless hours of driving along back roads, he said he had to get back to Garth.

"The M.A.O. is checking in Tuesday night, and the Dudleys and I have a lot to do to get ready for them."

"The what is checking in?"

"Massachusetts Amateur Ornithologists. They come to the outer Cape every year to watch the spring bird migration. This year there'll be about fifty of them, and with the third floor torn up, I don't know where we'll put them all."

Work at the hotel delayed him the next morning. We didn't even set out in the station wagon until after lunch. Thus it wasn't until late afternoon that, as we drove past one of the glacial age ponds south of

Orleans, I suddenly cried, "Look! In that field up ahead."

A donkey stood there, an old and shaggy one, tail switching, nose poked over a sagging split rail fence. Gabe said, in a taut voice, "Maybe."

We drove slowly past, staring at the donkey, who stared back at us from mild, long-lashed eyes. Had headlights startled him that rainy night? Could it have been his brays that came to my drug-altered senses as prolonged, two-note laughter?

I said, "There's a right turnoff just ahead. And we did turn right that night. I remember falling against the—the person's shoulder."

Not answering, Gabe made the turn, onto a road whose asphalt paving was broken and potholed in spots. On the right-hand side, the fenced meadow in which the donkey stood gave way to a stretch of pitch pines, and then to a neat, new little green ranch house, with a woman gathering newly opened daffodils from a flower bed beneath the picture window. After that, another stretch of pines.

When we came to it, the road's opening was so narrow that, if we hadn't been driving at the lowest possible speed, we'd probably not have seen it. "Turn right." My voice, coming from a restricted throat, sounded odd to my own ears.

That narrow road, with pine branches meeting above it, was already in twilight. After a few yards, it sloped downward to a rough plank bridge spanning a small stream. We drove over what now was just rattling boards, but which could have been the gigantic kettledrum of my nightmarish memories.

The road, rising now, ended in a cleared space on the brow of a low hill. To our left, at the foot of the weed-covered slope, stood a house.

It must have been standing there for at least two hundred years. Its roof sagged. Its warped brown shingles curled. As we approached it, wading through winter-killed grass and weeds, I was aware of the almost painful beating of the pulse in the hollow of my throat.

The porch was one step up. The door was secured with a chain and a padlock. The windows were covered by solid wooden shutters. Behind those shutters, small panes of glass?

Gabe said. "Wait here. I'll get in. I'll break open a cellar window if I have to."

He disappeared around the corner of the house. I waited, staring at a big lilac bush which stood, its buds still tightly curled, at one end of the porch. It was warm there in that sheltered spot, and silent. Except for the faint keening of a breeze through the dried weeds on the hillside, there was no sound.

After a while, from somewhere at the rear of the house, came the rasping protest of a nail, withdrawn from wood. The sound was repeated. Then, heart racing, I heard footsteps over a wooden floor, heard a window sash slide up. With a creak of rusty hinges, the window shutters at the left-hand side of the door parted.

"All right," Gabe said, in an odd, clipped voice. "Come in and take a look."

He helped me over the sill into musty-smelling warmth, and into what, until moments ago, must have been almost complete darkness. Now light from the window fell across ancient random-width floorboards, and an old table, its rough pine surface unpainted. On it stood a half-gallon jug of brown glass, with the remains of a candle stuck in its neck. A chair stood close to the table. Beyond those two rough pieces of furniture, a fireplace yawned in the opposite wall, its worn bricks bare of ashes.

I turned my gaze, almost fearfully, toward the end of the room where the black, raincoated figure had seemed to waver and change shape before my light-dazzled eyes. Despite the shuttered dimness there, I could see another rough chair, placed close to a window whose tiny panes, black against the shutters beyond them, gleamed dully.

"Yes," I said in a high thin voice. "Yes, this is the place he brought me to."

Gabe picked up the chair beside the table and carried it to the opened window. After a moment he said, "Remember telling me about that splinter that broke off in your hand, under the skin? Well, look."

I looked. A sliver of wood had been pulled free of the back edge of the seat. Its jagged tip was brownish with what I knew must be blood from my hand.

I raised my gaze to his face. There was excitement there, and anger, and something else. Relief. It told me that until this moment he hadn't been completely convinced that my experience had been real.

He said, "You climb back through the window. I'll close the shutters, and go out the way I came in."

"Through a cellar window?"

"A coal chute. It was boarded over, but the boards were rotten and easy to pull off. I'll hammer them back with a rock. Now go on. If we hurry, maybe we can get away from here before anyone sees us."

A few minutes later, as we drove from the sunny hillside into the gloom of the pines, he said, "The first thing to do is to find out who owns that house. Whoever took you there had a key to it. That doesn't prove he owns it, but it certainly points that way."

"Couldn't we ask that woman up the road, the one who was gathering flowers?"

Even before he answered, I realized my suggestion had been foolish. "And have her pick up the phone and say, 'I thought I should tell you, Mr. So-and-so, that some people today asked me who owns your house'? No, I'll drive to the county courthouse at Barnstable tomorrow morning, and look up the deed.

"Oh, hell," he added, "I can't go in the morning. A man who may buy the hotel is driving up from Yarmouth. But I can still get to Barnstable before the courthouse closes."

We stopped in Eastham for dinner. The food was excellent—we both had lobster—

but I was too keyed up to eat much of it. When we reached my place, Gabe came in with me. While I fed Howie, and turned him out for a stroll on the sand, Gabe closed and locked shutters, and turned window fasteners. As soon as Howie came lumbering back up the steps and into the house, Gabe kissed me good night.

"I'll call you as soon as I've looked up that deed. In the meantime, why don't you try to relax? Even your lipstick feels tense."

He waited out on the sun deck until he heard me lock the door. Then his footsteps went down the plank stairs.

Eighteen

"Relax," Gabe had said, and I wanted to, but my keyed-up state, plus the noise of the dogs over there in the swamp, made relaxation impossible. Perhaps because the moon was nearing its full, they were unusually vocal tonight, filling the air with yips, barks, and an occasional full-throated bay. To drown out their voices, I switched on the transistor, found everything on the dial too raucous, and switched it off. Taking *Quo Vadis?* from the bookcase, I began to read where I'd left off days before. The old-fashioned leisurely style, which at first had seemed charming, now irritated me, and so I replaced the book. But I had to have something besides that sagging-roofed house to occupy my thoughts, or I'd never relax sufficiently to sleep.

And then I thought of Laura's paperbacks.

I'd placed her hardcover books upright on the bookcase shelves, and stacked the paperbacks, lying on their sides, at one end of the row. Picking up several of them, I looked at the titles. *Dead Men Tell No Lies. Sleep Sweet, Sleep Long. They Murdered for Profit.*

Something wrong with that last one. The cover slanted down from the spine to the outer edge. Obviously some of its pages were missing. That seemed strange. Why should Laura buy a book—even a two-for-a-quarter book—in that condition?

Laying the other books aside, I opened *They Murdered for Profit.* The book seemed complete through page 170. But the pages from that point until page 181, where the last chapter began, had been ripped out. And with haste, apparently, because although the top two-thirds of the ripped-out section had come cleanly away from the binding, a ragged strip of margins still clung to the lower part of the spine.

I stood rigid, with Jules Laretta's words echoing through my memory. "She'd been burning something in the fireplace."

That missing chapter from this book? If so, perhaps she'd meant to burn the whole book. But even a paperback might resist the flames for a considerable time. And if she'd heard his jeep turning onto the gravel before his little house—

I imagined her swiftly ripping out those pages, dropping them onto the flames. Perhaps she'd had time to race to the bedroom, leave this book with the others, and, returning to the fireplace, stir the flaming pages so that they'd be consumed more rapidly. Then, when he'd opened the door, she'd told him, looking "white as a sheet," that she was ill, wanted to go home. And he'd never seen her again.

Praying that in her haste she hadn't thought of ripping out the table of contents, I turned to the front of the book. Yes, there was the list of chapters, a list so long that it was continued on the other side of the page.

Apparently the book recounted, in chronological order, true cases of those who had murdered out of greed. The first chapter was titled, "The Crusaders Were Their Victims." Perhaps that concerned the cruel twelfth-century ship's captains I learned of in a college history course, the ones who charged a stiff fee to take Crusaders to the Holy Land, and then left them to die on some barren Aegean island, while the ship returned to port for another load of victims.

Chapter Seven was titled, "The Innkeepers of Not-So-Merrie England." That, probably, was an account of the notorious country inns of Elizabethan times and later, where travelers were often murdered for their purses as they slept.

My eye hurried down the page. The title of Chapter Fourteen was, "Murder as Big Business." Capone-era gangsters? Perhaps. The next chapter, Fifteen, was called "The Bluebeard of Hollywood and Vine." I had no idea what that was about. Swiftly I turned the page. Then, motionless, I stared at the title of Chapter Sixteen, the missing one.

It was, "The Matrons of Maryfield, Mass."

Maryfield.

The black-coated figure beyond the screen of candlelight had asked, "What did Laurabelle tell you about Maryfield?"

And I, naturally enough, had answered, "She didn't. She never mentioned her."

A town. Not a woman. And Laura had known something about that town, something which the person in the raincoat feared she'd told me. Something important, dangerously important. When had Laura gained that knowledge? I felt sure that it had been only shortly before she burned those pages in Jules Laretta's fireplace.

I imagined her movements in his little house that afternoon. She must have chopped clams, and rendered salt pork, and sautéed onions to a pale yellow. At last, with the clam chowder simmering, she'd sat down, opened this book—and read something that had changed her whole life. It had sent her fleeing from her lover and from Garth, to hide herself under another name in a New York slum.

Yes, surely it had been this book. And, almost as surely, she'd had no previous inkling of the information it contained. Jules had said she had no secrets from him. Although that probably hadn't been literally true, it was still hard to imagine that she would have kept from him for long some deeply troubling knowledge.

In all probability, then, the discovery that had sent her white-faced and trembling from Jules Laretta's house was of some event that had occurred during her very early childhood, or perhaps before she was born.

If I could just get another copy of this book.

I turned to the title page, and saw with dismay that it had been published nine years ago, and that there was no mention of previous hardcover publication. Well, I realized now, the worn cover, and the brittleness of the pages, should have told me that the book was far from new. Only by a prolonged search would I have much chance of turning up another copy in some store that sold used paperbacks. True, I could write to the publisher. But my impression was that paperback publishers kept only their most popular books in stock year after year, and this one couldn't have been extremely popular, since I'd never heard of it.

What was more, even if the company did have this particular book in stock, days would pass before I'd receive it. And I wanted to know the contents of that missing chapter *now*. Surely it would tell me the reason for so much—not just Laura's puzzling flight and sudden death, but also my own nightmarish experience in that old house with the sagging roof.

There must be another and quicker way of finding out what had happened in

Maryfield, Massachusetts, on—

On what? What date?

With hands that shook a little I turned to the chapter which preceded the missing one, and skimmed through. It concerned a Hollywood bit player who'd married, and subsequently murdered, three well-off women. He'd died in the gas chamber at San Quentin in August, 1947. There were photographs of him, in the cowboy costume he'd worn in western films, and of two of his plump, smiling victims.

Swiftly I leafed through the book's last chapter, the one following the pages which had been torn out. It recounted the career of an English amusement park owner who twice had managed to dispose of heavily insured business partners. Again there were photographs of both him and his victims. He'd been convicted of murder in December, 1955.

The book still in my hand, I stared at the wall. Then sometime between the summer of 1947 and the end of 1955, some crime, spectacular enough to merit inclusion in this book, had been committed in Maryfield, Massachusetts.

Or was Maryfield a town? I'd never

heard of it. With dismay I realized that it could be almost anything—a country mansion, say, or a prison or hospital. And "Mass." didn't necessarily stand for Massachusetts. There must be other place names that began with those four letters. Just offhand, I could think of one. Massapequa, New York.

The road map in my car. It would tell me whether or not there was such a town in Massachusetts.

Unlocking the front door, I looked out. The nearly full moon cast a sparkling path over the tranquil water, and bathed the beach in a blue-white glow so bright that I could see distinctly a dark mass of seaweed washed up by the last high tide.

For a moment I hesitated, then turned back and got my car keys from my handbag. The morning after the rock throwing, Gabe had extracted from me a solemn promise not to "wander around at night." But it would take only two or three minutes for me to get down to my car and back. And surely, at this early hour, and through that flood of brilliant moonlight, no one would have tried to approach the house.

Nevertheless, as I descended the stairs and crossed toward my car, my senses were alert. But on this windless night I saw no movement, not even of the dune grass, nor the tall reeds stretching behind my house to the rising ground on which the pitch pines stood. And there was no sound except the faint crunch of my footsteps over the sand, and the distant baying of a dog somewhere in Joshua's Swamp. From the sound of him, he was at least part bloodhound.

Unlocking the car, I opened the glove compartment, and thrust my hand in. Driving gloves, a lead pencil, and facial tissues, but no map. When had I used it last? After a moment I remembered. It was during one of those solitary sightseeing tours I made my first few days on the Cape. I'd carried the map into a Provincetown restaurant, consulted it while I drank coffee, and refolded it. Then, apparently, I'd left it lying on the table.

Disconsolate, I realized that if I wanted to learn anything more tonight, I'd have to learn it from Gabe. And I hadn't wanted to consult him. He'd insist that I wait until he could accompany me to Maryfield, wherever it was. I saw no reason why I should wait. While he was showing the hotel to that prospective buyer and, later in the day, looking through deeds at the county seat, I could be finding out what those missing pages had contained.

I turned away from the car. As I reached the foot of the plank staircase I noticed for the first time that, just at the horizon, a dark band divided the sparkling bay from the moon-flooded sky. A fog bank lying out there. With the hope that it wouldn't sweep in to make driving difficult the next day, I climbed the stairs.

When Gabe heard my voice over the phone he asked sharply, "Anything wrong?"

"No, I'm fine. Gabe, have you got a road map handy, or an atlas?"

"Both."

"Would you look to see if there's a Maryfield, Massachusetts?"

"Sure." Then, in a quite different tone: "Maryfield!"

Swiftly I told him about the book with the missing chapter. He said, "Hang on. I'll be right back."

After a few minutes I heard the rattle of unfolding paper. "It's here, all right, about twenty-five miles the other side of Taunton."

"Does the atlas give its population?"

"Just a second. Here it is. At the last

census, the population was four hundred and fifteen."

In all probability, a village that small wouldn't have a newspaper. "What's the nearest fairly large town?"

"Well, about ten miles away there's a Hartley Falls. It's in medium-sized type on the map. And the atlas says— Just a minute. Here it is. Hartley Falls, twenty-five thousand." His voice quickened. "A town that size would have a daily paper. And anything that happened in a village only a few miles away would be big news in Hartley Falls. I mean, anything sensational that happened."

So his thoughts had taken the same direction as mine. "We'll drive to Hartley Falls day after tomorrow," he said, "and go to the newspaper office. It may take quite a while to look through several years of back files, but then, maybe we won't have to. Maybe we'll run into some staff member with a long memory."

"Perhaps."

We talked for a few minutes more, and then hung up. Even though I hadn't lied to him about my intentions—not in so many words—I felt a little guilty. But surely there'd be no danger in my taking a run up

227

to Hartley Falls. And I'd phone him when I was about halfway there. Otherwise, he might try to call me here, and become alarmed when I didn't answer.

I'd need plenty of sleep, if I intended to make a long drive the next day over unfamiliar roads. Once in bed, though, I found myself as wide awake as if it were high noon. At last I tried the old yoga trick of concentrating hard upon the spot just above the bridge of my nose. After a while the sound of Howie's snores seemed to dim, my thoughts blurred, and I slept.

Nineteen

The next day began anything but auspiciously. For one thing, the fog had rolled in during the night. I awoke to the drip of moisture from the eaves, and to the moans, like those of some recently bereaved sea monster, of a foghorn in the bay. Even worse, Howie was sick.

As usual, I'd let him out for his morning ramble. After a while I realized he'd been gone much longer than ever before. I hurried down the steps. And there, about forty feet away, the outlines of his barrel-like body blurred by the fog, he stood retching. When I approached him, he rolled his bloodshot eyes upward, and then was copiously sick.

Howie's digestion was aged and his greed

inordinate. He'd eat almost anything he could find. And so this was far from the first time he'd been sick. But he seemed much worse than ever before, his head hanging, his braced legs trembling. I'd have to get him to that vet whose sign I'd seen in Provincetown.

Leaving the house locked and shuttered, I loaded Howie into the car. It took me almost an hour to make the short drive to Provincetown, moving slowly through fog so thick that sometimes I couldn't see the roadside pines, and looking back frequently at Howie, blanket-wrapped and ominously quiet in the back seat. Was it just coincidence that Howie had become sick less than twenty-four hours after Gabe and I had found that old house? Probably. Still, it would have been easy for someone to have placed poisoned meat for him to find when I let him out for a few minutes the evening before. But there was no point in speculating until I heard what the veterinarian had to say.

The vet was a thin, genial man of about forty, with steel-rimmed glasses and ginger-colored hair. "So you up-chucked, did you, old boy?" he said to Howie. Then, to me: "What did you give him last night and this morning?"

As the vet lifted Howie onto the examining table, I mentioned the brand of dog food he'd had for dinner. "He's had nothing today as far as I know. I don't give him breakfast."

"Well, he doesn't seem to have any muscular soreness." As the vet prodded his sides, Howie feebly wagged his tail. "Better leave him here overnight. But I think he'll be okay."

I hesitated, and then asked, "Do you think he could have been poisoned?"

"Sure."

I said, appalled, "You mean there are people around here who—"

"Oh, I don't mean there are dog poisoners around. Just poisons. Insecticides, weed killers, that sort of thing. If a dog hunts, and gets hold of an animal that's loaded with the stuff—well, usually it doesn't kill him. It just makes him sick as a dog."

He had the air of a man who's just delivered a sure-fire line. I laughed dutifully and then said, "My dog isn't much of a hunter."

"Well, he probably picked up some moldy bread or something on the beach. Anyway, when you pick him up tomorrow,

I'm sure he'll be fine. Or call me this evening."

"I'm going off the Cape, and may not be back until late."

"Call me anytime up until one o'clock. I almost never go to bed before that."

"Thank you. Then I will call."

When I returned to Garth, I saw by the clock in front of the bank that it was almost eleven-thirty. Last night, I'd expected that by this time I'd be off the Cape and heading toward Hartley Falls. I drove into the gas station and asked Gene, the attendant, an almost tow-haired young man with a prominent Adam's apple, to fill the gas tank. "And could you give me a road map, please?"

While he filled the tank, I spread the map he'd given me on the steering wheel. I've never been any good at maps. All those numbers and symbols and lines confuse me. With the aid of the index on the reverse side of the map, though, I finally found Hartley Falls. I encircled it with a lead pencil, and then began to trace the route that would get me there.

"Hartley Falls, huh?" Gene had moved to my side of the car without my noticing it, and was now peering at the map. "You

232

going up there today?"

After a moment I said, "No."

His Adam's apple bobbed. "Why'd you put a circle around it, then?"

"It's where I'm going to turn off for Boston."

"That's not the quickest way to Boston! Here, let me show you—"

"I've heard the route through Hartley Falls is more scenic."

He stared at me. "Excuse me, Miss Warren, but you sure picked a fine day to look at scenery. You'll be lucky if you can see the white line down the center of the road. Well, that'll be four-twenty."

As I drove slowly along the rest of Garth's Main Street, I told myself what a fool I'd been. When he said, "Hartley Falls, huh?" why hadn't I answered simply, "Yes. How much do I owe you?" As it was, I'd fixed the conversation in his mind. I could imagine him saying to the next customer, or perhaps several customers, "You know that New York girl, the one that knew Laurabelle Crandall? Well, she's driving to Boston through all this fog and—get this!—she's going by Hartley Falls so she can look at the scenery."

Well, I thought grimly, it was too late to

worry about that now. In fact, the episode made it all the more important that I get to Hartley Falls—and back—as soon as possible. With any luck, I'd accomplish that before Gene's story reached someone for whom the words "Hartley Falls" might hold significance. And driving through this fog—sometimes so thin I thought sunlight might break through, other times so thick that even with my headlights on I could see only a yard or two—was going to require all my attention.

Soon after I crossed the Cape Cod Canal, the fog changed to rain. Gradually it thickened to almost cloudburst proportions, obscuring my vision as much as the fog had. At a roadside stand I stopped for a belated lunch, and to make a phone call to the Garth Hotel.

Mrs. Dudley answered. "Oh, Miss Warren. Gabe's just—wait a minute. Maybe I can catch him."

A few seconds later Gabe said, "Where the hell are you? I've been calling you and calling you. I was just about to drive over to your place."

"I'm on the other side of the canal."

"The canal!"

"Now wait, Gabe. I saw no reason why I

shouldn't drive to Hartley Falls while you're attending to other matters. By the way, did your prospective buyer show up?"

"Yes. Why couldn't you have waited—"

"Do you think he'll buy the hotel?"

"I think so," he said impatiently. "Now tell me why you started off alone in one of the worst fogs we've ever—"

"I told you why. What possible danger can there be in my driving up there?" No point in telling him of the episode at the gas station. There was nothing he could do about it, anymore than I could. It would just mean that two of us would be worrying, perhaps needlessly.

"Well, for one thing, there's all this fog."

"It isn't foggy here."

"You mean it's clear?"

"Well, not exactly. It's raining."

"Then be careful, for God's sake. And call me the minute you get back. No, don't call me. Stop here at the hotel. I'm going down to Barnstable to look up that deed, but I'll be back here long before you will."

"All right, I'll stop at the hotel."

I hung up after a moment, ate my lunch of underdone hamburger and overdone coffee, and drove on through rain so thick that sometimes the nozzle of a giant garden hose

235

seemed directed at my windshield. Mercifully, though, all but the last five miles of my route lay along parkways, so that at least I didn't have to cope with oncoming cars. But some of those that passed me threw such heavy sheets of rain water against my little car that it almost seemed to rock.

Around four o'clock, the downpour slackened to the proportions of a normal hard spring rain. By five-thirty, when I entered Hartley Falls, it had become a drizzle.

Hartley Falls looked like any small city at the end of the working day. Traffic was so heavy that, at two intersections, rain-caped policemen supplemented the traffic signals. Along the wet sidewalks, smeared with the reflections of neon shop signs, men and women hurried home through the drizzle.

Stopped by a red light, I cranked down the VW's window and spoke to the driver of the car next to mine. "Could you tell me where the newspaper offices are?"

"The *Evening Journal?* Just keep on the way you are for two more traffic lights. The *Journal's* three blocks beyond the second light, on the left side of the street."

I felt disappointed. I'd hoped that the

Hartley Falls paper would be a morning one, with a large and perhaps helpful staff still at work on tomorrow's edition. Well, surely there'd be someone in the office.

I found the *Journal* building, a four-story brick with a large bronze eagle over the door, easily enough. Parking space was another matter. All the spaces along Main Street were metered. I had no idea how long my search would take, and I didn't want to keep running down to the street every half hour to put another dime in the meter. Better to get off Main Street. I turned to my left.

The trouble was, other people had had the same idea. Before I found a space, I drove nearly two blocks, first past a few shops and offices that had spilled over from Main Street, then past big, turn-of-the-century houses whose lamplit windows bloomed softly through the rainy twilight. Leaving the car, I walked back to the *Journal* building.

Its double glass doors were locked.

I rattled the handle, and, after a moment, knocked on the glass. Soon an elderly man in tan coveralls came toward me, carrying a push broom. "Place is closed," he shouted through the glass.

"Please!" I shouted back.

After a moment he shrugged, leaned the push broom against the wall, and unlocked the door. "There's nobody here," he said. "You want to put in an ad? Come back tomorrow."

"I want to see someone on the staff."

"Staff goes home even before the business office closes. They come in at five in the morning, and quit at two."

"But there must be someone here!"

"Just Mr. Byles, the night editor."

"Well, can't I see him?"

Again he shrugged, and then stepped aside. "Fourth floor."

Despite its shiny plastic walls, the automatic elevator was an ancient one. It made a slow and shuddering ascent to the fourth floor, where its doors slid back with a grating sound. Directly opposite me, light spilled from a half-opened door onto the hallway's worn floor.

I pushed the door farther open. The room beyond was furnished with perhaps half a dozen desks, most of them holding upright typewriters, covered for the night. At the far side of the room, a man in a green eyeshade sat below a droplight, pecking away at a typewriter. As I moved

238

toward him he looked up, his thin face holding both surprise and irritation. "Yes?"

I'd hoped to find someone friendly and garrulous. Instead, this man probably had stomach ulcers, and almost certainly some deep grievance. Whether it concerned an extravagant wife, delinquent son, or his own thwarted ambitions, I had no way of knowing. But the grievance was plain in the deep lines bracketing his thin mouth, and in his curt, dry voice.

"May I look something up in your back files?"

"That department's closed." He began to peck at the typewriter. "Come back tomorrow morning."

"Is the door to the file room locked?"

"No, but the man in charge of it isn't here. Come back tomorrow."

"Please!" Hearing the thinness of my own voice, I knew that the long and difficult hours at the wheel had tired me more than I'd realized. "I've driven clear from the end of the Cape to find out something. Something important."

"What is it?" Obviously he asked, not out of a desire to be helpful, but to get rid of me as soon as possible.

"That's the trouble. I don't know. But I

have reason to think that years ago there was some sort of sensational murder in Maryfield."

"That's eight, nine miles from here. Better drive over there."

"But looking at a newspaper's files is the quickest way to find out. And I'm sure a town that small doesn't have a paper."

From his expression, I knew I was right about that. "This story you want to look up. When did it happen?"

"Around twenty years ago, I think. Maybe a little more."

"Well, I wouldn't know anything about that. I've been in this God-forsaken excuse for a town only five years. You'll have to come back tomorrow."

"Couldn't I look through the files myself?"

"Oh, all *right*." Shoving back his chair, he led me rapidly between the desks to a closed door set in the room's right-hand wall. Opening the door, he reached up. The glare of a droplight, set in motion by his impatient yank on its chain, swung over a long narrow table, flanked by tall stacks. Volumes about two and a half feet high, in dark red covers, filled the shelves.

"There it is, every edition of this rag

from nineteen thirty-four on."

Turning, he walked rapidly back to his desk. But he left the file room door wide open. That, I reflected wryly, must be so that he could pounce if I started to mutilate the files.

Twenty

I took down the volume labeled "June 1, 1947–December 31, 1947." It was heavy, and so coated with dust that I sneezed. Laying the volume on the table, I sat down and began turning pages.

Most of the banner headlines dealt with news of national or international importance. India and Pakistan Gain Independence. Partition of Palestine Voted by U.N. General Assembly. World Series Goes into Seventh Game. Now and then, though, the front page featured a local election, or a fire or robbery. Afraid that I might miss something pertinent to my search, I scanned the inside pages too, skipping only the sports news.

Dimly I was aware that in the big outer

room Mr. Byles' typewriter still clicked. Several times I heard the clatter of a news ticker, although I hadn't noticed such a machine as I crossed that room.

I toiled on through a second volume. Gandhi Assassinated. Soviets Blockade Berlin. Truman Elected to Second Term. Now and then the word "Maryfield" leapt out at me from some inside page. But each time it dealt with some minor matter, such as a Maryfield high school student winning a statewide essay contest, or Maryfield holding an election to determine whether or not the village would incorporate.

When I'd finished the back issues for the last half of 1948, I glanced at my watch. Almost eight. At this rate, I wouldn't get home until midnight, or perhaps much later if driving conditions were still bad. But I was determined to find what I sought, even if it meant that I'd still be here when the rest of the staff arrived at five in the morning. Returning the volume to the shelf, I took down the next one and carried it back to the table. Before I sat down I glanced into the city room. Mr. Byles was regarding me sourly from beneath his green eyeshade.

I kept turning pages. North Atlantic Pact

Signed. Russian Blockade of Berlin Lifted. In the outer room, Mr. Byles spoke softly into the phone. After several minutes of silence, I heard him say, "Thanks. Goodby." I turned another page.

Footsteps. I looked up to see him walking into the file room. He went to the stack and took down a volume. "I called a guy who's lived here since the Flood. He knew right away what you must be looking for."

Placing the volume none too gently on the table, he turned pages. I watched him, my heart pounding. "That it?" he asked, and shoved the open volume toward me along the table.

Laura's face looked up at me from the front page. And above it a black headline said: Police Allege Murder of Four Aged Patients at Maryfield Nursing Home.

"Well?" he asked.

Unable to speak, I looked up at him and nodded. My face must have been pale, because I saw a brief flicker of curiosity in his eyes. Then he said, "Wrap it up fast, will you? I don't like company when I work. That's why I took this lousy job." Turning, he walked out.

I forced my eyes down to the page. No, not Laura. This face was a few years older than the face I remembered, and the dark hair was curled under at the ends, not worn straight as Laura's always was. Otherwise the faces were almost identical. Beyond any doubt, I knew that this was a photograph of Laura's mother.

The caption read: "Mrs. Lorene Thompson, twenty-seven, younger of the two sisters being sought by the police."

So in those days Laura's mother had been Mrs. Thompson, not Crandall. Was Laura alive then? I looked up at the top of the page for the date. This edition had been published almost twenty-two years ago. Yes, Laura must have been alive then, but probably only a few months old. My gaze, shifting to a subhead, confirmed that. The subhead read: "Two Women and Infant Girl Are Object of Wide Search."

With a sense of inward shrinking, I read the story's opening paragraph: "A secret investigation carried on by this county's district attorney for the past few months yesterday resulted in warrants for the arrest of Miss Irene Adele Wade, thirty-two, and her sister, Mrs. Lorene Thompson, twenty-seven. Miss Wade is the founder and manager of the Maryfield Home for the Aged. Her sister has acted as the institution's head matron for the past six months. The two women have disappeared, along with the younger woman's infant daughter.

"The investigation was begun, according to County District Attorney Clayton L. Smith, after his office received a tip from a discharged employee of the home. The informant, a practical nurse, alleged that the elder of the two missing women had recently murdered an eighty-year-old woman patient by holding a pillow over her face. The informant also stated, according to Mr. Smith, that even if Miss Wade's sister hadn't participated in the alleged crime, she 'must have known about it.'

"Moving quietly over the past three months, county authorities have exhumed the bodies of four other patients who have died at the nursing home during the past year. In three cases, the district attorney's office states, traces of arsenic were found."

Still with that sense of revulsion, I read on. In each of the cases investigated, the aged woman had been without friends, and with no relatives closer than second cousins. Shortly before death, too, each of the old women had willed her possessions— twenty thousand dollars and some diamond jewelry in one case, lesser sums in the others—to the nursing home's founder, Irene Adele Wade.

The final paragraphs read: "Miss Wade, believed to have been a native of Pennsylvania, came to Maryfield five years ago. With the aid of a mortgage issued by the Hartley Falls Savings Bank, she bought a large farmhouse with several outbuildings a mile from Maryfield, and converted the property into a nursing home. Six months ago her sister joined the staff. According to employees of the home, the younger woman's husband had been killed in a car crash a month before his infant daughter was born.

"Authorities are also questioning Dr. Percy Hines, who in each of the cases investigated had issued a certificate giving 'cardiac arrest' as the cause of death.

"Apparently because they had learned of their impending arrest, the two women fled the Maryfield Home sometime after midnight last Tuesday. District Attorney Smith states that he hasn't yet discovered who tipped the fugitives off.

"As of now, no trace of the missing women has been found."

Lifting my eyes from the page, I stared at the row of tall red volumes in the stack. I was almost certain that I knew where the sisters had gone. Canada. There, using false names, they'd taken advantage of Canada's almost incredibly lax passport laws to obtain passports. They'd gone to France. And there Ed Newcombe, a visiting American with only a few years to live, had fallen for the older sister's cold good looks.

Why had the two sisters decided to risk returning to the state from which they'd fled? Perhaps they were low in funds. If so, Ed Newcombe, wealthy and respectable, would have been a great temptation to them. Perhaps, too, after the lapse of more than a year, they'd felt fairly safe. And then there was the younger woman's illness. Probably aware that she had only months to live, she might well have wanted to establish her child in comfortable surroundings before her death. Anyway, they'd come to Garth as Mrs. Newcombe, Mrs. Crandall, and Mrs. Crandall's two-year-old daughter, Laurabelle.

And then, almost twenty years later, Laurabelle had opened a used paperback book—

What must she have felt as she saw a face almost identical with her own staring up at her? For surely, since the book's other chapters had been illustrated with drawings and photographs, the missing chapter must have been also, and probably with this same photograph.

Perhaps the photograph alone would have been enough to convince her of the identity of the "Matrons of Maryfield," especially if she'd seen a copy of it in her mother's or aunt's possession. But perhaps she'd also recognized other details in that chapter, which surely had been a far more thorough account of the case than the hastily written news story I'd just read. Perhaps there'd been a description of a distinguishing birthmark, or of a piece of jewelry still in her aunt's possession.

She'd burned those pages, told her lover she felt sick—I could imagine how she must have felt sick to the depths of her—and driven home to face her aunt. Mrs. Newcombe probably had responded to the hysterical girl with a flat denial that she'd ever even heard of the Maryfield Home for the Aged. Perhaps later she'd admitted her identity, but denied that either she or her sister were guilty of the crimes for which they'd almost been arrested. And perhaps, still later, she'd said coldly, "There's nothing you can do about it now except bring the worst sort of trouble on me and on yourself. If you've got any sense at all, you'll forget you ever saw that book."

The next day Laurabelle had fled to New York. No wonder that her gray eyes had looked haunted. No wonder that she—niece of a woman who'd murdered coldly and viciously, daughter of a woman who at best was accessory after the fact of murder—no wonder that she was determined never to marry, never to pass along her heritage to another human being.

Returning my attention to the volume before me, I looked rapidly through perhaps a dozen more editions of the newspaper. For a few days the story had remained front-page news, with headlines like *More Exhumations Ordered by D.A.*, or, *Search for Missing Women Now Nationwide*. Then the story dropped back to the inside pages. One of them said that later exhumations, unlike the first five, had revealed no evidence of foul play. Another dealt with an unconfirmed rumor, recounted by an employee of the nursing home, that the older sister had an illegitimate child, "a young son," whom she'd placed "with friends." Still another said that all suspects taken into custody so far had been released as innocent.

Getting up, I walked over to the stack on

legs that felt a bit unsteady, and replaced the volume on the shelf.

As I entered the city room, Mr. Byles looked up and asked, "Finished?"

Nodding, I managed to say, "Thanks."

Again I saw that faint curiosity in his eyes. But all he said was "So long," and returned his attention to his typewriter.

Twenty–one

As the elevator made its shuddering descent, I wondered whether or not to telephone Gabe. No, I decided, it would take a very long phone call indeed to convey to him what I had learned. Besides, it still wasn't quite nine o'clock. If the weather had improved—

It had, tremendously. As I stepped from the building I looked up and saw ragged clouds, driven by strong wind currents in the upper air, scudding across a sky already flooded by the light of the rising moon. With such driving conditions, I could zip back to Garth in a third of the time it had taken me to get here.

Turning left at the corner, I moved up the quiet side street, past the closed shops and then the well-kept houses, many of them showing the blue glow of a television set through their windows now. In the middle of the second block, I crossed to where I'd left my car parked beside a giant maple whose branches, their buds starting to unfurl, stirred in the breeze. Standing in the street, I opened my handbag. Vaguely aware of a car approaching from the direction of Main Street, I took out my key container. The key in my hand, I glanced at the oncoming car.

Perhaps it had already started to swerve toward me, although in that first instant I wasn't consciously aware of any deviation in the headlights' path. In fact, it *must* have started to swerve. Surely it wasn't pure intuition that sent me dodging around the front end of the Volkswagen a split second before the car roared past, with only inches separating its right side from the left side of my car. In one terrible instant, visualizing what would have happened if I hadn't moved, I knew the fragile vulnerability of my own body, with its crushable flesh, its shatterable bone, its blood that even now could have been running along this quiet, tree-lined street.

I clung to the car's hood, telling myself I

mustn't faint. I must turn my head, look. The car might be coming back.

It wasn't, at least not yet. The twin taillights, already two blocks away or more, were dwindling in the darkness.

Somehow I got behind the wheel, started the engine, made a U-turn. I drove back to Main Street, turned right, and, in the middle of the block, guided my car into a parking space before a brightly lighted drugstore. Then I crossed my arms on the steering wheel and sank my head upon them. After a while my gasps and shudders ceased, and I was able to straighten up.

I thought, staring at the pedestrians who moved along the sidewalk, shall I go to the police? Tell them that someone had tried to kill me with his car?

They'd ask, "Who was he?" and I'd have to answer that I didn't know. They'd ask me to describe the car, and beyond replying that it was a sedan, I wouldn't be able to. I'd had the impression that it was a black car, and fairly old, but it might have been a dark shade of green, or blue, or even red. And of course I didn't know its license number.

Before long, someone at the police station would say, "Are you sure it wasn't an accident? Cars can go out of control, you know."

The only way to convince them it wasn't an accident would be to tell them everything. Laura's death. My own drugged and sightless ride to that old farmhouse. The rock that had crashed into my living room. All of it. And it wouldn't sound convincing to them, any more than it had to Chief Jones. Perhaps it would sound even less so. Still in a state of shock from having been literally inches from death, I wouldn't be able to give a calm and orderly account.

But if Gabe backed me up, they might be convinced.

Of course! That was the thing to do. Call Gabe. Perhaps he'd start driving here immediately. Or perhaps we'd decide that it was best for me to go to the police here in Hartley Falls. He could call them in about twenty minutes, to back up what I'd told them. I walked into the drugstore and entered a phone booth. With fingers that still shook, I dropped a coin in the slot and then dialed.

Within a few moments I was hearing Mrs. Dudley's voice. It sounded oddly harassed. "Gabe's not here, Miss Warren. He phoned from somewhere near Barnstable more than an hour ago. Something went wrong with his car, and he's having it fixed in a garage. He left a message for you, though. He'd like you to wait for him here at the hotel."

I asked, feeling dismayed, "Did he mention the name of the garage?"

"No. He just said it was near Barnstable."

"Well, thank you, Mrs. Dudley."

I hung up and then just sat there, my hand still on the phone. Should I go to a hotel? The thought of spending the night in a Hartley Falls hotel, sleepless inside a locked room, made everything within me shrink. Locked hotel rooms could be entered, by means of a passkey, or through a fire escape. Or a voice on the other side of the door could say, "May I speak to you, Miss Warren? It's the manager," when it wasn't the manager at all.

I yearned for the safety of the Garth hotel, and of my own shuttered and Yale-locked little house, with its gun in the bedside stand.

If I were careful, perhaps I could get there tonight—safely. In fact, now that some of the shock had worn off, and I could think more clearly, I realized that probably there was little need even to be careful. The driver who'd tried to kill me couldn't know that I'd observed so little of his car. For all he knew, I'd be able to give a good description of it, including part or even all of its license number. The chances were overwhelming that he wouldn't stay behind the wheel of that car any longer than he had to. Perhaps he'd already abandoned it.

And even if he were still in it, would he use his car tonight for another attempt upon my life? Try to run my car off the road, at this still-early hour, on a well-traveled highway? That was most unlikely. The risk would be great, and his chance of success small. Even if he did cause me to crash, the odds were that my injuries would be less than fatal.

Another reassuring thought was that the five-mile stretch of road connecting Hartley Falls with the parkway, and the parkway itself, would be crowded now. In addition to the usual evening traffic, there'd be motorists who'd postponed or interrupted their travel because of the wretched driving conditions earlier.

Still, I'd be careful, very careful.

Returning to my car, I backed it out of the parking space and retraced my way

257

through Hartley Falls. As I'd expected, the traffic on the two-way highway beyond was of almost rush-hour proportions. Sandwiched in between a white station wagon and a yellow sports car, I drove the five miles. Despite my reasoning of a few minutes before, I found myself tensing whenever the headlights of some impatient motorist, moving out to the left-hand lane to pass, showed in my rear-view mirror.

At the turnoff, the white station wagon kept straight ahead. Speeding up to narrow the gap between my car and a red convertible, I followed it onto the turnoff.

As I'd hoped, the parkway was reassuringly crowded. Nevertheless, when a curve in the road showed me a patrol car about sixty yards ahead, I felt a surge of joyful relief. Passing two cars, I swung back into the right-hand lane, directly behind the patrol car. With my headlights bathing that blessed word, "Police," painted in big letters on the car's trunk, I could at last turn my thoughts to my assailant's identity.

Who'd been driving that car which, if I hadn't dodged, would have killed me, just as surely as Laura had been killed? Obviously it was someone who, guessing my purpose, had followed me to Hartley Falls, someone who knew what I'd find in the *Journal* files, and who had waited for my exit from the building. He was also someone desperately determined that I not pass along the knowledge I'd gained.

To whom would it be the most important that I be silenced? Adele Newcombe, obviously. But that driver couldn't have been she, a woman who'd recently suffered a stroke—

Sudden realization made me let up on the throttle, so that the VW bucked. Who could be sure Adele Newcombe had suffered a "slight stroke"? There was only her word for it, hers and Dr. Rainey's.

True, there was that faint lisp in her speech. But that could be faked. So could that slight droop at one corner of her mouth. A bit of transparent tape, placed farther back along the jawline to draw the corner of the mouth downward, would be sufficient. With her own doctor spreading the word that she'd suffered a stroke, who would doubt it?

Dr. Rainey. What had been the name of the doctor who'd signed those death certificates at the nursing home? Oh, yes. Percy Hines. I wondered what had happened to him after he'd been questioned by the district attorney. Had he been completely exonerated? Deprived of his license for malpractice? Indicted for complicity in the deaths of the aged patients?

Now I realized that I should have spent at least another hour in that file room, reading carefully those follow-up stories I'd just skimmed through. And I should have searched the issues covering events of at least several weeks after the two sisters disappeared. There might have been items about minor figures in the case, such as the person who'd tipped off the police about the old woman who'd been smothered with a pillow. Reading that part of the story, I'd felt fleetingly that it reminded me of some-one. But eager to learn what the next para-graph held, I'd read on, and now I couldn't recall who or what I'd been reminded of.

Too, there was that unconfirmed rumor that the elder sister had had "a young son." How young? Fifteen? Almost certainly no older than that, considering Adele New-combe's age at the time, and probably younger. Whatever his age then, by now, if he were still alive, he'd be—

My thoughts, and even the blood in my veins, seemed to stand still for an instant.

That car. A dark sedan. It had swung in

close behind me. Very close. Only the driver in the front seat. I narrowed the space between myself and the police car.

The sedan speeded up slightly.

Oh, God! Had my reasoning been all wrong? Was the person who sought my death so desperate that he would draw alongside me now, and shoot at my head? In my mind's eye I saw my own car out of control, crashing into the police car, or perhaps swerving into the path of some oncoming car. In the confusion, the sedan and that dark figure behind its steering wheel would have at least a chance to escape. Whereas if I lived—and, oh, how could I have been so muddleheaded as not to realize it until now!—Adele Newcombe would surely stand trial for the murder of those old women.

The sedan was moving toward the left-hand lane now, to draw alongside my own car. Desperately, I pressed the VW's horn, and at the same instant thought, "The window!" It was down on my side. A shot from a gun equipped with a silencer wouldn't even be heard. With my left hand, I frantically cranked up the window.

The car was in the other lane now, and slowly drawing alongside. With an effort, I jerked my head around to face the driver, who in another instant would bend forward to get a good view of me—

A child's face stared at me through the sedan's right-hand front window. A sleepy-eyed blond girl of about three, so small that, until now, I hadn't known she was there.

The sedan moved past me, past the patrol car, and returned to the right-hand lane.

Too shaken to drive, I turned off onto the grass and stopped. So did the patrol car. Both uniformed men got out, and walked toward me.

"Were you blowing your horn at us, miss?" He was about thirty-five, with a polite voice.

"Yes." I should have said no. I should have said I'd sounded the horn accidentally.

"Why?"

"I—I was afraid."

"Afraid of what?"

"Of—of the car that just passed."

"That old sedan with a kid in it?"

"I didn't know there was a kid in it. I thought—you see, someone—someone in Hartley Falls tried to run me down. In the street."

He exchanged glances with the other officer, a slightly younger man. "You mean deliberately?" When I nodded, he asked, "Did you report this to the Hartley Falls police?"

"No."

He smiled slightly. "Then you must not have been sure it was deliberate."

Still trembling, and with no hope of giving in a few minutes, here at the roadside, any adequate explanation, I remained silent.

The younger man touched his companion's arm. "Just a minute, Mel."

Moving away from the car, they exchanged a few low-voiced words, and then walked back to me. The older man asked, in a more serious voice, "Have you got some good reason to be afraid? Somebody been threatening you? I mean, maybe you had a bad fight with your husband, or your boy friend."

I seized upon the explanation. "My—my ex-husband."

"You want to sign a complaint against him? We'll take you to—"

"Oh, no! I'm much better now. I've just been—very upset, and I'm still nervous. So if you'll just let me keep following your car—" My voice trailed off.

"All right," he said, after a moment.

263

Then, sternly: "But no tailgating. You were tailgating us a few minutes ago."

"I'll stay back."

"And another thing. Since you won't make a charge against anyone, you're not an official part of our job. I mean, if some hyped-up character goes past at seventy miles an hour, we'll take out after him. And don't you even try to keep up."

"I won't."

"And anyway, we patrol this road only as far as the next sub-station. That's about fifteen miles from here."

The younger man said, "We could turn her over to Joe and Harry." Then, to me: "How far you going?"

"To Garth, up on the Cape."

"Well, the next patrol car goes as far as the canal. Once you're on the Cape—well, that's not heavily patrolled this time of year. But if you wait at a sub-station, you'll pick up a patrol sooner or later."

As they turned toward the car, the older man said, "Now, remember. If some hyped-up character—"

"I'll remember."

No hyped-up character came along. At the legal limit, we drove to the next sub-station. Parking the VW on the gravel,

I waited while Mel and his partner spoke briefly to two other officers, already seated in a second patrol car. Grinning slightly, the man behind the wheel glanced at me.

That was all right. Let them speculate about my fight with my ex-husband all they pleased, as long as they allowed me to stay close to them.

After a moment the driver started his engine, and made a "come on" gesture to me. Behind the patrol car, I moved back onto the parkway. The night had grown colder, I noticed, now that the last of the cloud cover had blown away. I switched on the heater.

Keeping far enough back that I couldn't be accused of tailgating, and yet close enough to discourage other cars from crowding in ahead of me, I followed the patrol car. Perhaps it was the moonlight, blue-white on the well-drained parkway, which except for an occasional inch or so of water in an underpass, was now dry. Perhaps it was the pendulum of my emotions, swinging away from the terror of that moment when the black sedan had started to pass me. Anyway, I not only felt safe; I felt triumphant, in a grim sort of way. Very soon I'd be with Gabe. Between us, we'd

see that the person, the unspeakable someone, who'd left Laura's broken body on a
New York street, and later tried to crush
me like an insect against my own car, got
everything that was coming to him.

When the patrol car and I were about ten
miles away from the Cape Cod Canal, some
suicidal psycho in a yellow sedan flashed by
us at perhaps eighty miles an hour. Like a
whippet breaking from the starting gate,
the patrol car took off.

Despite my new confidence, I felt more
than a little uneasy. What should I do now?
Continue on across the canal, and then stop
at the next sub-station? The very thought of
being questioned by still another policeman
filled me with dismay. Better hurry to the
next exit, I decided, and find some busy,
well-lighted place where I could think it
over.

Only minutes later, an exit sign loomed
up. I turned off onto the long, ramplike
curve. At its foot, I looked up a four-lane
highway and saw, about a hundred yards
away, a diner spilling light from its windows onto a graveled parking space. As I
approached it I saw that the parking space
held half a dozen passenger cars, a panel
truck, and an enormous diesel truck with a

266

van trailer. I turned into the parking lot and stopped beside the diesel. On its trailer, almost the size of a boxcar, were the words "Cape Cod Van Lines."

Inspiration struck me. I hurried into the diner, to be met by the wail of a juke box and the smell of freshly made coffee. Among the customers who'd chosen the counter rather than the booths were two men with Teamsters' Union badges fastened to their caps. The truck driver who sat near the entrance was of average size. He couldn't be the one. It would take someone as brawny as the man sitting at one end of the counter to handle that truck and trailer.

I walked over to him. "Excuse me, but are you the driver of that big van outside?"

The brown eyes he turned toward me looked pleased, startled, and a little wary.

"Yes, ma'am." The voice was southern. Like the voices of many big men, it was also shy.

"Are you driving onto the Cape tonight?"

"Clear to Provincetown."

"Would you mind if I stayed with you as far as Garth? My car's only a Volkswagen, but I'll drive as fast as I can."

267

"That would probably be too fast for me, ma'am. I can't go over the legal limit. Company rules. But you're real welcome to stay close to my rig, if you want to."

His big square face was filled with the questions he was too shy, and perhaps too polite, to ask. I said, "You see, I think someone's been—following me."

He said, with shocked indignation, "That's a downright mean trick, bothering a girl who's driving alone at night. What kind of a car is he in?"

"A black sedan, fairly old."

"All right. You drive ahead of me. If I see a car like that acting funny—trailing close behind us, I mean—I'll give you three blasts on the horn, and we'll both stop. He'll have to go on then. If he don't, I'll deal with him. How far you say you're going?"

"Garth. But I wouldn't expect you to leave the highway at the Garth exit, and then go to all the trouble of getting back on."

"Ma'am, I'll take you right into Garth. The old road runs through there. I can keep on it the rest of the way to Provincetown."

I had a quick cup of coffee, while he finished his steak and French fries. Then my denim-clad Galahad and I went out into the crisp spring night.

I drove the rest of the way across the canal and up the moon-flooded Cape highway without incident, and without fear. It's remarkable how safe you can feel with the headlights of a twelve-ton truck, driven by a two-hundred-pound man, always visible in your rear-view mirror. But I'd also begun to feel tired, tired to the bone, more tired than I'd thought possible. And I was hungry. Since breakfast that morning, I'd had nothing but one thin hamburger. Well, there'd be food at the hotel, even though at this hour, almost midnight, Gabe or I would have to cook it. And after I'd eaten, and we'd talked, I'd go up to one of the second-floor rooms, and then take a bath in that old-fashioned public bathroom. After that, I'd sleep and sleep.

Followed by the rumbling diesel, I made the Garth turnoff, drove a few miles along the pine-bordered side road, and entered the town. The lights were just blinking off in Steve and Grace's Tavern.

Seconds later, I frowned in bewilderment. As usual at this hour, Main Street was dark and silent. But from the start of the business district on, both sides of the street were lined with parked cars. What on earth—?

Then I remembered. The Massachusetts Amateur Ornithologists. No wonder Mrs. Dudley had sounded harassed when I phoned her from Hartley Falls. All these people were about to descend upon her, or perhaps had already descended, and Gabe hadn't been there to supervise.

As for me, I felt an absurd impulse to break down and cry. No room at the inn. Not for me. Every available room would be taken. And probably I couldn't cook any food there, not without causing great inconvenience. The Dudleys must have already set dining room tables, and perhaps made preliminary preparations in the kitchen, against the early hour when a horde of outdoor types would descend for breakfast.

There was a parking space, just beyond the Town Hall. Switching on my turn signal, I slid into the space, and then leaned out of the car to wave "Thank you." With a "You're welcome" blast of its horn, the huge truck and trailer rumbled on down the dark street.

Wearily getting out of the car, I walked the rest of the way to the hotel.

Twenty-two

The situation was even worse than I'd anticipated. Some of the amateur ornithologists didn't have rooms either. Three middle-aged women, an elderly man, and a young couple with a married look about them sat in the lobby. Except for the girl, all of them looked irritated and sleepy. She was already asleep, sitting on a leather settee with her head on the young man's shoulder. Mrs. Dudley, standing behind the reception desk, wore a fixed, anxious smile. I walked over to her and asked, in a low voice, "Is Gabe here?"

"He was. But he's gone out again to try to find rooms for these people. He thinks the Tarringtons might put some of them up, and Miss Carruthers, and the Bakers."

"When did he leave?"

"About ten minutes ago."

So it might be as long as an hour before he returned to the hotel. At the thought of waiting for him here in one of those lobby chairs, each of my frayed nerves and tired muscles cried out in protest. My locked and shuttered little fortress, with its bathtub and well-stocked refrigerator and comfortable bed, seemed to me like Paradise. But it would be foolhardy to try to get there alone, over a dark and deserted country road.

"Has Mr. Dudley gone to bed yet?"

"No, he's in the kitchen, slicing ham for tomorrow's breakfast."

"Do you think he'd go with me in the pickup truck over to my place? It wouldn't take him long. I'm so very tired, and yet I don't want to drive out there alone at this time of night."

She said sympathetically, "I don't blame you, what with somebody throwing a rock through your window." She didn't mention the earlier experience that had sent me to Chief Jones, although she must have heard about it. Perhaps she felt that was best passed over in tactful silence. "I'll go ask Jim. I'm sure he'll drive over there."

He did, following my car over narrow

roads lighted only by the moon. Leaving his truck parked beside my little bug, he climbed with me to my front door. I said, inserting a key into the Yale lock, "Would you mind waiting while I check through the house?"

As soon as I'd turned on the living room light, I went into the bedroom and looked in the nightstand drawer. Yes, the gun was there. While Mr. Dudley waited, I made sure that all the shutters and windows were still locked. Then, feeling a little foolish, I looked into the bathroom, the clothes closet, and even the narrow broom closet in the kitchen.

"Everything's all right, Mr. Dudley. Thanks a lot."

"That's okay. You want Gabe to call you yet tonight?"

"Please ask him to." Tired as I was, I wanted to talk to Gabe.

When Mr. Dudley had gone, I went into the bedroom and hung up my coat. As I turned away from the closet my gaze fell on Howie's pallet. Call anytime up until one, the vet had said. One o'clock was still a few minutes away.

The vet answered on the second ring. Howie, he told me, was fine. "He had another sick spell after you left, but that was all to the good. I was able to make sure he hadn't gotten hold of any poison."

Yes, it was good to know that Howie had been the victim of nothing except his indiscriminate greed.

"You can pick him up anytime tomorrow," the vet added.

"I will. And thank you very much."

I hung up, and headed straight for the kitchen. I'd skip the bath. Just scrambled eggs and bacon and hot coffee, and then bed.

I'd finished my belated supper, and was drying the plate I'd used, when I heard a car stop out there between the dunes. My nerves tightened with mingled anxiety and expectation. Gabe? Had he decided to drive over rather than phone?

Then, as I heard the expensive-sounding slam of a heavy car door, followed by Senator Carberry's booming voice, I felt only exasperation. "Now I'm sure it'll be all right, Mrs. Yerxa," the Senator was saying. "You and Oscar can spend the night with me, and tomorrow—" His voice became inaudible.

I threw the dishtowel onto the sinkboard. He was promising those politically important friends of his that tomorrow they'd have their own little hideaway, right on the bay. And the sunsets, Mrs. Yerxa, the sunsets! Well, I thought grimly, we'd see about that. We'd agreed that I was to have this house for four weeks. Besides, with the only hotel in town full, where could I move to in the morning?

He was climbing the steps now. He knocked. "Miss Warren?"

Swiftly I crossed the living room, opened the door. "Yes, Senator?"

"I'm sorry to disturb you at this hour, but I was by earlier, and you weren't here. And I must talk to you about something."

The smile on his noble-Roman face was tense. The Presidency, I thought, hangs in the balance.

"If it's about my giving up this place—"

"It is, Miss Warren." He lowered his voice. "These friends of mine have arrived earlier than I expected. I'd promised them the place, and they had no way of knowing I'd rented it to—"

"Couldn't we talk tomorrow? I'm very tired."

"But it will take only a minute to explain it to you! I'm not asking you to sleep on the beach, Miss Warren. I'll see to it that you have other accommodations."

From the car parked up by the dunes came a woman's laugh, followed by the murmur of a man's voice.

I couldn't go on standing there, my tired body beginning to shiver in the chill night air. The sooner I let him speak his piece, the sooner he and his bigshot friends would drive off. I opened the door wider. "Come in." A moment later I said, sinking wearily into one of the wicker chairs, "Won't you sit down?"

When he'd sat down on the edge of a wicker settee, I asked, "What sort of accommodations?"

"Very nice, much nicer than this place. It's over on the ocean side of the Cape, and rents for five hundred a month during the season. I'm agent for it, and I'll let you have it for what you're paying here. It's completely furnished, and today I had the utilities turned on and the place stocked with linens. You could take your suitcases over there right now, if you wanted to. In fact, that's—"

The phone rang. "Excuse me," I said, and moved eagerly toward it. Back turned to the Senator, I lifted the handset.

It was Gabe. I asked, "Did you find

276

rooms for those people?"

"Finally. Bird watchers! Remind me to kick the next robin I see. How about you? The Dudleys said you looked completely beat."

"I am, but otherwise I'm all right."

"I know you must be too tired to talk about it tonight, but did you find out anything in Hartley Falls?"

"A great deal." Aware of my landlord's listening ears, I added, "I'll tell you all about it tomorrow."

"All right. I'll ring off in a minute. But I want to tell you what I found out at the county seat. Now this isn't conclusive, of course. Somebody else could have a key to that old house. But anyway, guess who bought it about eight months ago."

I said tautly, "Please, Gabe. Just tell me."

"Lucius P. Carberry."

After a moment he said, "Jane! Are you still there?"

"Yes."

Could Carberry tell, sitting over there only a few feet away, that the hair on the back of my neck had prickled? Had he heard his own name? He must have, I thought, aware of the panicky quickening

277

of my blood. Gabe had been speaking loudly and distinctly.

"You sound sort of funny," Gabe said.

There might be a gun leveled at my spine right now, my spine which seemed to be shrinking away from my vulnerable flesh. If I said the wrong thing—

"I'm just terribly tired."

"All right," Gabe said, after a moment. "I'll call you in the morning. Good night, Janie."

He hung up. The instant I heard the click, I knew—with my stomach a tight knot, my heart drumming—that I should have managed to say something, anything, that would bring him here. No use to think about that now. And don't look around. Just get into the bedroom. "Excuse me," I said. Aware of little fear ripples down my back, my legs, I walked into the bedroom. I opened the little drawer, snatched out the gun.

Invisible beyond the partly closed door, he said, "Miss Warren." His voice sounded thin.

"Yes."

"Come in here, Miss Warren. It's no use. I heard most of what Gabe said. And forget the gun. I was in this house earlier tonight, and took the bullets out."

Of course. My landlord, with his own key. Pointing the gun at the bedroom rug, I released the safety, and then pulled the trigger. The gun clicked. Just clicked.

"Leave the gun there, Miss Warren, and come in here."

I looked at the bedroom window. Locked tight. And beyond the glass, the fastened shutters. My fortress, now a prison. The only quick way out would be through the kitchen door, with its ten-foot drop to the sand below. And to reach the kitchen, I'd have to go through the living room. I dropped the gun on the bed, and walked through the doorway.

He still sat there on the edge of the settee. His right hand, holding a gun, rested on his knee. His face was very pale. The lamplight glistened on his glasses, and on his broad, sweat-beaded forehead.

Halting beside the wicker table, I clutched its edge with one hand. "Why?" My lips felt wooden, clumsy.

"It's not my fault. None of it. I want to make that clear to you. Everything's the fault of that woman, that horrible, horrible woman."

I moved my numb lips. "Mrs. Newcombe?"

The big head nodded. "Years ago I was—infatuated with her. She kept hinting at some scandal in her past. I think it amused her to see just how uneasy she could make me and yet keep me bound to her. Anyway, in one of my letters to her—my foolish, foolish letters—I said that even if she'd committed murder, I wanted to marry her. Of course, in those days I didn't know she'd actually—" He broke off.

A weak man, frightened and self-loathing, and therefore doubly dangerous with a gun in his hand. Don't even glance toward the kitchen doorway, I ordered myself. Just try to keep him talking.

"Then you didn't know she'd killed those old women?"

"I swear I didn't, not until after Laurabelle ran away. Adele Newcombe called me to her house then, and told me the whole hideous thing. She said she didn't trust Laurabelle's promise to keep quiet. She said it was up to me to do something about it. If Laurabelle did talk, she'd take that letter of mine out of her safety deposit box. Everyone would know I'd wanted to divorce my wife for a—"

Again he broke off. Through the open kitchen window came the sound of several voices, raised in argument. Not people down there in the Chrysler. A car radio, tuned to one of those late-night talk shows.

He was speaking again, his voice feverish. "And I want you to know that what happened to Laurabelle wasn't my fault either. Not really. That woman had located her through a detective agency. She ordered me to go down to New York and threaten Laurabelle, tell her that if she ever talked, some hired gunman would— Oh, God! That—that creature, forcing me to act like some Mafia hood—"

I said, "Senator Carberry."

At that title of which he was so proud, a spasm crossed his face. "Yes?"

"Do you mind if I sit down?"

"No." Grotesquely, he smiled.

Trying to keep all expression out of my face, I crossed in front of him to a wicker armchair that stood beside the kitchen doorway. When I'd sat down, I said, "You —you can't use that gun, not here, in a house you own—"

I saw his knuckles whiten slightly as his hand tightened around the gun. "Not here. I never intended to do it here. I didn't want

281

to leave any—sign of a struggle." His voice was dull now. "I thought if I could get you to come willingly down to my car, I could hit you over the head with this gun, take you someplace else—"

"You mustn't—kill me anyplace. A man like you—"

"I have to. Don't you see? If you tell what you found out in Hartley Falls today, everything will come out, even—about Laurabelle—"

"I've already told. I went to the Hartley Falls police."

He shook his massive head. "No, you didn't. You're a bad liar, Miss Warren. It shows in your face. Besides, I was in Hartley Falls today, too. I know when you—dodged away from me on that side street, and when you drove out of Hartley Falls. You hadn't had time to tell a long story like that to the police."

I said nothing. After a moment he went on, in a flat voice, "But if you stay alive, you'll tell. That's why I have to do this. It's not just myself I'm trying to save. It's three hundred years."

I knew what he meant. The three hundred years that the Carberry name had been one of the most honored ones on the Cape.

He looked down at the floor. "Three hundred years!" he repeated.

I moved then, grasping the arm of the wicker chair even as I rose from it. I whirled, hurling the light chair at him with all the strength I could muster. That gun went off, but whether he'd aimed it or fired it by accident, I didn't know. By that time, I was in the darkened kitchen, twisting the key in the lock. I opened the door onto chill moonlight, and jumped.

Twenty-three

I'd remembered to bend my knees to lessen the shock, but even so, my right ankle turned as I landed in the soft sand. Only dimly aware of pain, I ran a few yards down the slight slope, plunged almost headlong into the tall reeds of the marsh, and then, after threshing my way forward for a few seconds, lay flat and motionless on the soggy ground.

In the house behind me, quick, heavy footsteps crossed the kitchen. He must be standing in the kitchen doorway now, looking out. Instinctively trying to press my body deep into the soft ground, and unmindful of the chill that struck through my clothing, I held my breath. I hadn't dared to stay on my feet long enough to penetrate more than a few yards into the marsh. If he too jumped, and then kept straight ahead, he'd find me within seconds. But surely, oh, surely, he'd be afraid to jump. He was more than twice my age, and overweight. He'd be afraid of breaking a leg.

Fleetingly I became aware of a grotesque sound. Up in the parked Chrysler, the murmur of voices had given way to an automobile commercial, with a girl singer demanding that a winner lead the way.

Footsteps retreating rapidly across the kitchen now. He was heading for the front door and the stairs to the beach. I scrambled erect. Hating that cold, revealing moonlight, I moved as rapidly as I could, not toward the black pines that concealed the swamp, but on a slanting line to the left.

Enough! He must be at the foot of the stairs by now, and turning toward the corner of the house. I dropped, full length.

For an interval, there was no sound except the thud of my own heart, and the keening of a vagrant night wind through the reeds. He must be standing at the sand's edge now, scanning the expanse of moonlight-bleached reeds for a dark, telltale scar. I said a prayer of thanks for the wind.

Surely his eyes were darting now here, now there, as a clump of reeds bent to the wind and then stood erect. For a fleeting moment I realized that to him the reed-covered marsh must look like the photographic negative of a wind-ruffled lake, with the water light in color, and the whitecaps black.

A crackle of reeds. But to my right, thank God! He'd decided the chances were that I'd moved straight ahead into the marsh. How long would he thrash around out there, that overweight, hysterically frightened man? How long before he would hurry to his Chrysler and drive, perhaps sobbing—where? To Adele Newcombe's? Down the highway leading off the Cape? Across the Cape to the towering cliffs above Nauset Beach?

He was directly to my right now, and only a few yards away. I stopped breathing. After a few moments I exhaled, slowly, silently. The thrashing sound was a bit farther to the right now. He'd turned toward the road.

Something cold and slimy and tiny-clawed landed on the back of my hand. A frog, I realized an instant later, but by then the damage had been done. I'd let out a small cry. Reeds had crackled as I'd flung my hand and arm sideways to rid myself of the loathsome little creature.

The thrashing sound stopped. I heard a shot, and, simultaneously, a whistling noise just above my head through the reeds. Then again the crackle of reeds, drawing closer.

I got to my feet, turned, and, bent almost double, plunged back across the marsh toward the beach. I had a lead of about thirty feet, and I could move faster than he could. Maybe I could get into the house, lock the door. I'd be a clear target for a few seconds as I crossed the sand to turn the corner of the house, but I had to risk it. Even with him lumbering after me, death in his hand, I couldn't force myself to run toward the pines, and the swamp, and the lurking dark shapes.

A bullet sang past. Not close. He was a bad shot. Was his the kind of gun that held only six bullets? I had no idea. But if it was, he'd already used three.

My right foot plunged up to the calf in cold mud. Impetus carried me a step farther, and my left foot sank even deeper. Only a mudhole, with firmer ground a step or so beyond? Or a wide slough separating this part of the marsh from the beach?

I couldn't risk it, I thought despairingly, couldn't risk becoming a mired, helpless target. The mud made a sucking sound as I withdrew my left foot, then my right. I turned, still crouched, and started on a leftward slanting line toward the pines.

He must have been saving his shots. For at least a minute there was no sound except the crackle of my flight through the reeds, and his pursuit. Then another shot, closer this time.

The pines were only a few yards away. Run, I thought, run! Straightening, I darted toward that black line of trees. Another shot, so close that I felt, or imagined I felt, the wind of its passing. Then the ground was suddenly firm underfoot. A few more steps over rising ground, with my body braced for a bullet's impact. Then I was in the shadow of the first line of trees, the second, the third. After the flooding moonlight, the woods seemed almost totally dark. Stumbling over something—a root, probably, I fell to one knee.

I froze. Twin green lights, a little below the level of my own eyes, somewhere ahead in the darkness.

Slowly, carefully, I got to my feet and

pressed close to a tree trunk, trying to quiet the sound of my ragged breath. No green lights now. Had the dog retreated deeper into the woods, back toward the swamp? Or was it circling, silently, to get between me and the marsh?

Footsteps, not running now, only a little way to my right. Praying that no twig would break underfoot, I moved to the other side of the tree trunk.

Carberry halted, so close that I could hear his sobbing breath. No other sound at all, for perhaps a minute. Then the snap of a twig, and then another and another, as he moved deeper into the trees. My eyes, more accustomed to the dim light now, caught a glimpse of him—the tall, heavy body, the mane of white hair. Then he was gone.

I turned. Safe, now. Oh, almost surely, safe.

Somewhere deeper in the woods, snarls and yelps and a deep-throated baying rose in a sudden, hideous chorus. I heard a hoarse shout, and the crack of a bullet. Then he was screaming—

Without remembering how I got there, I found myself, facing the wood, on the firm ground just outside the first line of trees. Dimly I was aware my throat felt raw. And then I realized that I'd been adding my own screams, scream after scream, to the chorus of screams and snarls issuing from the woods.

I heard no crackling sound through the reeds behind me. Just his voice. "Jane!" He was beside me now, a rifle in the crook of his right arm. "What is it?"

I must have pointed, and perhaps said "Carberry," because Gabe ran, shouting, toward that terrible uproar. After a moment I heard the rifle crack several times. The screaming stopped. The snarling and yipping also ceased for a moment, and then began again, farther away, at last dwindling to one defiant bark.

"Jane?" Gabe's voice, from somewhere beyond the first line of trees.

"Yes?"

"Get to the phone." His voice sounded labored. "Call Jones. Tear up sheets or something for bandages." I could see him dimly now, that heavy body in his arms.

I turned, and plunged back across the reeds.

Twenty-four

I helped carry him up the plank stairs, holding his legs while Gabe supported his shoulders and moaning, tossing head. In the living room, under the glare of the overhead light, we lowered him to the carpet. Gabe threw an approving glance at the articles I'd assembled while he struggled through the reeds with his heavy burden. I'd placed scissors, antiseptic, a bath sponge, and a water-filled basin on the wicker table, together with a sheet from which I'd already torn a few strips.

"Jones on his way?"

"His assistant said he'd locate him. He'll also call an ambulance. From Eastham, I think he said." Then: "Oh, Gabe! If only I'd known you were on your way here!"

"I kept thinking how strange you'd sounded over the phone. Finally I put my rifle in the station wagon and drove over."

He'd knelt on the floor by then, and, with the scissors, had begun to slit the torn trousers. Kneeling beside him, I dipped a sponge into water.

Luke Carberry was fully conscious, but he'd been badly bitten on the legs, and on the torso too, to judge from the blood soaking through his white shirt. Somehow, though, he'd managed to ward off the springing animals from his throat and face. Miraculously his horn-rimmed glasses had stayed in place. Behind them, tears seeped from his closed eyes as he turned his head from side to side.

Gabe said grimly, "While I was carrying him here, he told me he'd tried to kill you."

"He tried twice. He almost succeeded in running me down in Hartley Falls tonight."

As I told him about that, and what I'd learned at the *Journal*'s office earlier, Gabe's face became even grimmer. But his hands kept busy, raising the wounded man to a sitting position, so that he could ease his torn jacket from him, and scissoring away the blood-soaked shirt. I too worked, bathing the ugly wounds and applying antiseptic and bandages.

"Adele Newcombe was blackmailing him," I said, "with a letter he'd written to her years ago. She ordered him to go down to New York and threaten Laurabelle. Instead, he killed her in the street."

Gabe sat back on his heels. "Mr. Carberry."

The blurred gray eyes behind the hornrims opened and then closed.

"I don't think you're too badly hurt," Gabe went on coldly, "but you might be. Anyway, don't you think it would be a good idea to tell us all you can?"

The pale lips shook. "Yes. I want to tell you."

"About the car in which you ran Laurabelle down—"

"It was a rented car. You see, I—I didn't want people to know I was going to New York. I drove to Hyannisport, and flew from there to Boston. I rented a car in Boston, under another name, and drove to New York."

The hoarse, hopeless voice went on, describing how in New York that cold March night he'd found a parking space a block and a half away from Laura's apartment. When he rang the bell under the name "Laura Crane" in the apartment house foyer, there'd been no response. He'd returned to his car to wait. Around midnight he saw a dark-haired girl of about her height approaching the apartment house from the other direction. Getting out of his car, he hurried to meet her.

"It was Laurabelle, all right. She—she looked terrified, and sort of—revolted when she saw me. Before I could stop her, she ran up the steps and went inside. After about a minute I started pushing her bell, but she didn't press the buzzer to unlock the downstairs door. I could see how she might look horrified at the sight of someone who reminded her of Garth, and the things that terrible aunt of hers had done. But I felt that maybe it was more than that. Maybe she'd guessed I'd come down here to threaten her—"

Not knowing what else to do, he'd returned to the parked car. As he sat there, he became more and more certain that the girl was phoning the police. Soon he'd see an official car draw up outside her apartment, its red roof light revolving.

Frightened, he'd started the engine of the rented car, intending to get out of the neighborhood as soon as possible. And at that moment Laura had come out of her apartment house and hurried away in the other direction.

At first he felt only relief. So she hadn't called the police, after all. Moving away from the curb, he started down the street after her. Then it came to him that she might be on her way to some nearby police station.

"At the corner she turned to cross the street. I suddenly thought, 'If she were dead, I wouldn't have to worry anymore.' And then my foot pressed hard on the throttle—" His big head turned from side to side on the carpet. "The—the impact. It was awful, awful!"

He'd sped north, and finally stopped in a Bronx gas station which was closed for the night. With its water hose he'd washed off the bent bumper and crumpled left fender. Driving still farther, he'd stopped at a motel in Westchester. The next day in Hartford, Connecticut, he'd had his car repaired, telling the garage attendant that someone had backed into him. He'd driven the car to Boston after that, returned it to the car rental agency, and flown back to the Cape.

"I felt wretched, wretched. But at least I

thought that woman wouldn't make any more demands upon me, now that she knew I'd—now that she knew Laurabelle was dead. Then you turned up here, a friend of Laurabelle's, and Adele wasn't sure you were as ignorant as you seemed—"

I said, "She planned your taking me off the beach that night, didn't she?"

"Yes."

He described how she'd told him in detail how to drug me, and what questions to ask me. To each of his protests, she had an answer. In all probability, she said, I wouldn't go to the police. After such an experience, I'd be too frightened, too doubtful of my own sanity. Probably I'd run straight back to New York. And if I did tell Chief Jones or anyone else, I wouldn't be believed. What's more, if I set out to find that old house, I'd never succeed. How could I, when I'd been taken there drugged, and unable to see?

She'd reasoned well, I thought fleetingly. How could she have foreseen that a donkey's bray, sounding to me like sardonic laughter, would sink deep into my drugged consciousness?

"What did you use?" Gabe asked. "LSD?"

Eyes squeezed shut, he nodded.

"Where did you get it?"

"A—a legislative committee at the State-house studied drugs a few months ago. I was on the committee. These doctors and social workers turned drug samples over to us—"

He began to weep again, the tears running unchecked down his pale face. He'd been so proud of his office, so hopeful, as he probably would have put it in a speech, that the people of his great state would summon him to even higher service.

This weak, vain, foolish man had killed my friend. He'd tried to kill me. And yet as I looked down at him, I found I couldn't hate him.

Gabe must have been feeling something of what I felt, because when he spoke his voice was almost gentle. "You won't have to talk much longer." He paused. "You threw that rock, of course."

"Yes." His swollen eyes shifted to me. "I had this sort of desperate hope that I could frighten you off, before you and Gabe found that house."

Gabe asked, "Did you know we did find it?"

Carberry's voice was dull, as if it no

longer mattered. "Not until tonight, when I heard you two talking on the phone."

"How did you know Jane had gone to Hartley Falls today?"

"The kid in the service station told me, when I drove in there about noon."

He'd started after me, he said. I could imagine him driving the big car recklessly through the gray smother. After he'd driven more than an hour without seeing my car, he decided that I must have turned off onto another route, or perhaps parked my easily overlooked little car among larger ones at some roadside restaurant. Anyway, he was sure he'd missed me. At an even faster rate, he'd driven on to Hartley Falls, and left the Chrysler in a garage there.

Gabe asked, "You rented another car?"

"I bought an old one, for spot cash, in a used car lot." He drew a ragged breath. "That salesman took so long, so damned long, to make out the bill of sale and change the registration slip to the name I gave him. It was a false name, of course."

He'd parked the old car near the *Journal* building and waited, hoping that I hadn't reached Hartley Falls yet, and that he could stop me somehow if I started to go into the building. Finally he'd been forced to the

298

conclusion that I might already be inside. He'd gone to the entrance and pounded until the janitor had appeared. Yes, the janitor said, a young lady had gone upstairs nearly an hour ago. "But I can't let you go up, mister. There's just that old crab of a night editor up there. He'll probably chew me out plenty for letting the girl go up."

Feeling that there was at least a chance I wouldn't discuss whatever I learned from the back files with the "old crab," nor ask to use his phone, Carberry had set out to look for my Volkswagen. He'd soon found it, parked on that side street. Driving back along that same street, he'd parked on the other side of its intersection with Main Street, so that he could see me as soon as I left the newspaper building.

"I—I already had a gun with me. If you'd turned toward that drugstore a few doors away, maybe I'd have followed you in to try to keep you from phoning anyone. Maybe I'd have risked letting you know I had a gun and ordered you to walk out quietly. But instead you walked the other way, toward where you left your car parked."

He began to cry again, very quietly. Gabe asked, "Where's the old car you bought?"

"I just left it a few blocks farther up, on that same side street."

He'd been almost in despair by that time, knowing that his one hope, a slim one, was to stop me before I talked to Gabe or anyone else. On foot, he hurried to the garage where he'd left his Chrysler. Driving at high speed, he'd passed my VW, one of a group of slow-moving cars, on the five-mile stretch that connected Hartley Falls with the parkway. I must have actually seen his car pass, I realized now. But, with my senses strained for the sound and sight of an old black sedan, his car probably had registered upon my consciousness only as a big gray one.

For a while his luck had held. In Garth he'd risked stopping at the hotel, and found the lobby filled with bird watchers. A distracted Mrs. Dudley had told him that Gabe was in a garage somewhere down the Cape, having his car fixed. That buoyed his hopes that, even if I'd tried to get in touch with Gabe, I hadn't been able to.

Sure that my little bug was at least still half an hour from Garth, and probably more than that, he'd driven to my place and let himself in with his own key. ("If I had to," he said, looking at me with wretched eyes, "I was prepared to shoot that dog of yours," and I answered, "He's at the vet's.") He found my gun, and emptied it. He'd even used my phone. Disguising his voice, he'd called the hotel and asked for "Mr. Harmon." Mrs. Dudley, sounding more distracted than ever, told him that Mr. Harmon had just left, "to try to find room for six guests."

Carberry had been sure that finding rooms in Garth for six people would take at least an hour, and probably much longer. He'd felt almost as sure that I, physically and nervously exhausted, wouldn't choose to wait in a hotel lobby with irritated strangers and an overwrought housekeeper. I'd leave a message for Gabe, and drive to my rented house.

Descending the plank stairs, he'd driven back along the beach road to where it met the wider one. He'd parked on the wider road a hundred feet or so beyond the intersection, and waited. He'd had a bad few minutes after he'd seen my car, followed by Mr. Dudley's truck, turn onto the beach road. For all he knew, I'd asked Mr. Dudley to wait with me until Gabe arrived.

"But after a while I saw the truck come back up the road and turn toward Garth. I waited until the truck was out of sight. Then I tuned the radio to one of those talk shows, so that when I got here you'd think that—that Oscar Yerxa—"

After he'd spoken the name of his influential friend his throat must have closed up, because he said nothing more. In the silence, I heard a car coming down the beach road. It stopped outside. "Chief Jones," Gabe said.

I nodded. Crossing the room, I opened the door, and saw Chief Jones starting up the plank steps. Just as he reached the sun deck, I heard the far-away wail of an ambulance siren.

Twenty-five

As I said in the beginning, one recent afternoon I drove down the Cape for a last look at the old house with the sagging roof. If I could see it now, I'd reasoned, when I was both safe and happy, maybe it would lose some of its nightmare quality. Maybe it would seem much like any other old house.

And after a while, as I sat there in the warm May silence, broken only by bird song and a bumblebee's hum, it did begin to look like any other old house. Before long some couple—but not Gabe and I, not us!—with a taste for old houses and enough money for restoration would buy it from Lucius Carberry's estate.

Yes, he's dead. Not of his wounds. The doctors didn't consider those too serious,

303

once he'd been given a rabies shot. But a few hours after he was taken to the hospital, he suffered a mild heart attack, and two weeks later a massive and fatal one. If there is any way at all that heart attacks can be self-induced, I think his were. Certainly he must have felt that nothing which awaited him beyond the hospital doors was worth the effort of breathing in and out.

But at least, I thought, as I started my car and turned it toward the tunnel-like track through the pines, at least he'd had one satisfaction before he died. He'd dictated and signed a bitter statement concerning Adele Newcombe's blackmail of him.

Mrs. Newcombe's still alive. Alive and well in the Bristol County Jail, awaiting trial. Because of the especially abhorrent nature of the crimes with which she's charged, and because she evaded arrest on those charges for so many years, she's been denied bail.

She's kept silent, of course, about the events of twenty years ago at the nursing home in Maryfield. But she did issue one public statement through her no doubt embarrassed lawyer. It concerned the newly revived rumor that she'd had an illegitimate son. Despite the legal language in which it was couched, what it boiled down to was: she'd never had a child, particularly an illegitimate one, and how could people be stupid enough to think that she, Irene Adele Newcombe, had ever let any man make a fool of her.

I'd reached the fenced meadow where the donkey grazed—yes, he was still there— and had turned toward Garth, when Bill Brockton's old Jaguar, its top down, drew alongside my car. "Hi, there," he said.

At the moment there was no other traffic. We stopped our cars side by side in the road. He said, gazing at me through glasses that glittered in the sunlight, "You still going to marry that guy?"

"That's right. Next week. And we're going to New York as soon as the sale of the hotel is completed."

"You're making a terrible mistake. He's a Cosa Nostra bigshot, you know. So were his father and grandfather. The family name is really Harmonini."

"Well, we all have our little faults. I'd better go now. I have an argument with Gabe to finish."

"It's over nothing trivial, I hope."

"My driftwood collection. Gabe moved it all from the beach cottage to the hotel for me, but he wants to leave most of it behind when we go to New York. Any household, he says, should be able to struggle along with a half-dozen pieces of driftwood."

"You see? It's these little temperamental differences that foreshadow serious trouble ahead."

I looked in the rear-view mirror at an approaching farm truck. "Bill, we're blocking traffic."

He said, easing his car forward, "As soon as you realize you can't stand him any longer, look me up."

"I'll do that."

I looked after the Jaguar. Such a nice man, Bill. Pray heaven he'd never know it had even crossed my mind that he might be Adele Newcombe's son. And pray heaven even harder he'd never know that, for a few terrible seconds on the parkway that night, I'd expected to see his face looking across at me from that old black sedan.

I let the farm truck rattle past. Then, smiling, I drove on toward the hotel, and Gabe.

The publishers hope that this
Large Print Book has brought
you pleasurable reading.
Each title is designed to make
the text as easy to see as possible.
G.K. Hall Large Print Books are
available from your library and
your local bookstore. Or you can
receive information on upcoming
and current Large Print Books by
mail and order directly from the
publisher. Just send your name
and address to:

G.K. Hall & Co.
70 Lincoln Street
Boston, Mass. 02111

or call, toll-free:

1-800-343-2806

A note on the text
Large print edition designed by
Bernadette Montalvo.
Composed in 18 pt Plantin
on a Xyvision 300/Linotron 202N
by Genevieve Connell
of G.K. Hall & Co.